_A_ CANDLELIGHT ROMANCE

CANDLELIGHT ROMANCES

THE
WATCHING
WINDOWS

Ruth McCarthy Sears

A CANDLELIGHT ROMANCE

Published by
DELL PUBLISHING CO., INC.
750 Third Avenue
New York, New York 10017

CHAPTER 1

I certainly never expected Charles Christian to remember me, but here we were, facing each other
across the piano in a San Francisco drawing room
where someone was playing "If I Loved You" from
Carousel, and Charles was beaming at me with dawn-
ing recognition, his nice mouth moving in the words
of the sentimental song.

I wouldn't even have been here in this expansive
place with its gorgeous view of the Bay if it hadn't
been for BJ and her less-pretentious studio in the
basement of the San Francisco apartment building
atop Nob Hill. She had asked me to stay with her in
her cluttered digs while I was getting my bearings.

"Good address," she said, leading me past the furnace room and into one dreary room with a murky
north light. "I mean, there *are* rats coming up from
the waterfront, but they seem quite indifferent—unless you antagonize them or something. By the way,
we're invited to a bash upstairs tonight, so unpack
something devastating in a hurry."

I was tired from the long train ride from Kansas
City—yes, train! I couldn't afford plane fare, much
less hotel accommodations, and someone—a patient,
I think—had given me BJ's address, along with the
information that she was a successful commercial
artist. There were buckets of paint, stained tarpaulins,

and sketchy charcoals cluttering the narrow premises, but other than that dismal evidence of poor house-keeping, there was nothing to bear out this statement. I didn't know BJ well enough to question her, so I washed in the grimy bowl in a corner, wishing with all my heart for a cleansing shower, which my hostess told me was in use at the moment and only available in the early morning or late at night.

While I was dressing, BJ lacquered her nails in a desultory fashion and filled me in on our mutual friends from Abilene High back in Kansas. Not that *her* friends were exactly mine, even at home, for BJ was what is known as "sophisticated" in Abilene, and even if I had run around in the same crowd, I would have been scared to death and completely mystified by their brittle wit and conversation.

"Oh, and Raphael Gibbs—his name was Clarence, or Chester, or something at home— Anyway, he's some sort of faith healer now down on the peninsula, and pulling in disciples by the dozens, so I hear. Remember him?"

I shuddered. I remembered Clarence with unadulterated horror. He wore thick glasses that made his eyes look like pinpoints, and he had a mean little mouth and mousy hair. All of which was not his fault, and neither was it the reason for my inordinate dislike for him. But one day, hunting crawdads along Mud Creek with my brother Matt, we had come upon Clarence cruelly dissecting a live frog. The frog's suffering was bad enough, but the expression on Clarence's face was more awful, and it haunted me for months even though Matt had beat Clarence up and killed the frog mercifully with a rock.

I really didn't want to go to the party. I supposed it would be in some hovel like BJ's, with hippie types sitting around on the floor expounding about the war in Vietnam and tearing the Government to shreds. Matt had died in that war, and I liked to think that he had died honorably, believing in a just cause. Anyway, it still hurt to remember what a clean-cut, candid, and idealistic boy he had been. We had been very close, since we lived on a heavily mortgaged farm, and were largely dependent on each other for companionship after our parents' untimely deaths. The farm went to pay their creditors eventually, and because I was already in training at St. Joseph's Hospital in Kansas City, Matt had announced his intention of joining the Air Force. We had spent one summer evening together in Swope Park listening to the band concert and saying our solemn goodbyes—and that was the end for us.

It was a long time before I reconciled myself to Matt's death. I had no one after that. No mail ever came to me at the nurses' dormitory; no phone messages were for me. I lived in a vacuum of complete friendlessness that next year until graduation. Later, I rallied, of course—and hurled myself into my career with such avid enthusiasm that I came to Dr. Burley's attention.

Dr. Burley was from Abilene, too, and of the same generation as my parents, both of whom he had known. He had spoken to me kindly many times, and a month ago he had called me into his office and asked me how I would like to come to San Francisco.

"Mrs. Regent is a very frail woman of dwindling means, I'm told," he said, his eyes crinkling under bushy brows. "She lives in a remote spot on the coast some distance from San Francisco and, probably for that reason, is unable to keep a nurse. It occurred to me, Miss Carewe, that since you have no one of your own, you might enjoy being on private duty and in a home."

In my youthful dedication, I thought, *I'd like to be kind to someone who needs me and, perhaps, come to love them very much.*

Actually, that was what decided me—that, and a desire to see the far West. Love was what I needed, and the sterile halls of the hospital discouraged anything but service. The love that I had meant to bring into my career, the personal attention to my patients, had been dissipated by ordinary common sense after a while. You couldn't sit holding hands with them and draw them out of their post-operative doldrums by listening to confidences while lights were winking up and down the corridors for your attention. There were pills to give to kill the pain, bedtime bromides to bring, pillows to fluff and blankets to straighten, and often not a personal word was spoken during these ministrations. It was a cold world of prime duty, and at the time Dr. Burley mentioned the new assignment, I was considerably disillusioned about the nursing profession.

"Mrs. Regent was once a concert pianist of some renown," Dr. Burley went on. "She injured her back while riding in Spain many years ago, and my colleague, Dr. Davidson, cared for her while he lived." He held up a letter. "This is from his son, Michael, who seems to have considerable interest in Mrs. Regent."

"You mean he lives with her?"

The doctor shook his head. "Between lecture tours, he might possibly visit her, yes, but according to this, he has just returned from Majorca and has found her in a pitiful condition." He thrust the letter into my hands. "His San Francisco address and telephone number are here, and he promises to drive you down to Regent Manor on the first of April. Shall I write him that you will come?"

I had set out with mixed spirits, emotionally and economically. I suppose I could have borrowed money from Dr. Burley, but with my next check being mailed to Mr. Davidson and BJ kindly offering to take me in, I could manage within reason.

Now with Charles Christian moving around the piano toward me, I could only think tritely, "Small world!"

I had seen him many times in Kansas City, had read his name in the social columns of the *Kansas City Star,* and had entertained a normal curiosity about him. His family's country home was just off the bus route where I passed going to town on my afternoons off to shop or see a movie. It had paddocks, surrounded by white fences, horses, and a racing arena where I frequently saw the trainers timing and exercising the high-spirited animals. There were finely bred dogs, too, with the plumy tails and soft muzzles of setters, both English and red Irish. The house was set apart on a knoll, gleaming white, wide and majestic, with imposing pillars. I often watched for it, always thinking of Matt, the born farmer, and how he would have loved having a place like that. In fact, when I first saw Charles, he reminded me so nostalgically of Matt that I could only stammer in reply to his question.

The bus had broken down within the line of vision from the grand white house. Small figures up beyond appeared one by one, to point and gesticulate until, presently, one of them detached himself and came down the poplar-lined lane, where we sat fanning ourselves in the heat and waiting for the driver's clumsy attempts to get the vehicle going again.

Charles spoke to me because I was closer than the other passengers: "What's wrong?"

I stammered and shrugged without giving him a

definite answer. I couldn't have. He looked so much like Matt, so slim and tall and sun-bronzed, so kind and clean and wholesome, that I was tongue-tied. He went to the front of the bus, where the driver was jiggling things and swearing under his breath, and peered under the hood.

I couldn't take my eyes off Charles, and when he pulled his head out from the massive hood he smiled directly at me apologetically. "Not a bit of use!" he said. "The motor's done for."

His intonation was slightly British, and the voice not at all like Matt's, which dissipated the illusion and restored my poise partially. "But I'm on duty in half an hour," I protested. "At the hospital—St. Joseph's."

He took my elbow. "Come on up to the house, then," he said matter-of-factly. "I'll phone for another bus, then run you out to St. Joseph's myself."

There were other people in the house—servants, I suppose, and an elderly dignified man, who came into the entry hall and asked, "What is it, Charles? Flat tire?" His bright-blue eyes rested on me absently, and Charles said, "Dad, this is one of the nurses from St. Joseph's. Miss —?"

"Carewe," I said quickly. "Marly Carewe."

Mr. Christian nodded and returned to a discussion of the bus's malfunction with his son. Finally, he agreed to place a call to the bus company and Charles led me outside to a small foreign car that looked like an oversize bullet. He helped me in, calling to a mixed group lounging around the pool that he would be back in seconds.

Awed by the sleek appointments and performance of the car, I said nothing until we were well outside the gates and off the lane. Then I glanced at his face, and he was smiling at me in that disconcerting boyish way that reminded me of Matt.

"So you're a nurse," he said in evident admiration. "Remind me to get sick sometime."

It was so friendly and unpremeditated that I laughed. "You look perfectly healthy."

"So do you, and very pretty," he said. "Tell me, what's it like pandering to a lot of peevish invalids? Do you get bored?"

Bored and lonely, I could have said. But I did not want pity from this nice, lively boy, nor sympathy, either, for my impecunious state that made it necessary for me to make my own living.

"There are interesting times," I said brightly, "and interesting patients, too. We have a new research laboratory."

"Yes, I noticed that when I first came home. I've been in England this past year." He said "bean," and I was duly impressed. "Tell me, what is that bubble on top with the light?"

"Oh, that's the cobalt wing. It's new, too, this past year."

He regarded me with interest. "I say, you sound English—are you?"

I wanted very much to be just then. My father had been a London Carewe, but the ancestry was not particularly impressive that I had heard. He had come to this country as a youth to find a way of making a living and had met my mother and started farming. That was the sum and substance of it, but I was not about to give the mundane details to this fascinating man who seemed desperately to want me to be English.

"Yes," I said, "I am."

"I knew it!" he exclaimed, delighted with his own perception. "That same tawny hair and blooming complexion. I say," he said, extending his hand, "it's good to find someone from the Isles." I took his hand, enjoying the contact of pressure and warmth, and he went on, "I've been rather at loose ends, you know, since I returned. Do you notice a rather brassy quality to American pronunciation?"

"I've been here a long time. I daresay I've grown accustomed to it."

"Rath-er! But it's nice to meet you, Miss Carewe— a nurse and all that, you know. Do you have time off now and then? I'd like to take you for a drive some evening."

I glanced surreptitiously at my watch and saw that there was no time to pursue this fascinating exchange if I were to report for duty on time.

"You—might call me sometime," I said demurely, "if you wish. I'm in the nurses' dormitory—Marly Carewe."

He let out a typically American whistle that sounded strange after all the British tones. "Will do, Marly, real soon. And don't turn me down, you hear? I've got my pride, you know."

His pride, however, did not prompt him to call me for another month or so. We went for a lovely drive along country lanes toward Sedalia and stopped at a wayside inn. We laughed a lot, and Charles sang with the radio in a strong, clear voice, his profile very appealing in the moonlight.

When we were saying good night under the glare of the overhead light at the dorm, his eyes lingered on my mouth and he said, "I'd like awfully to kiss you, Marly, but not here. Next time—would you mind?"

But there was no next time. The phone in the hall shrilled for other girls, but not for me. And after a while, I had almost forgotten Charles Christian, except when I passed his home on the bus. Nearly a year had gone by.

"Molly Cruse," he said now, his breath warm on my cheek, "as I live and breathe. What are you doing 'way out here?"

"Hello, Charles," I said composedly. "And it's Mar-ly—M-a-r-l-y—Carewe. C-a-r-e-w-e."

"All right," he laughed, "so I goofed." His accent was not so pronounced now, I noticed. "What in the name of thunder are you doing in San Francisco?"

"That's a long story," I said suggestively. I couldn't see eating scrambled eggs in BJ's apartment. Perhaps he would ask me to dinner. He did immediately.

BJ's eyebrows lifted knowingly when I asked if she minded. "Go ahead, darling—that's the purpose of these bashes. You do work fast, though, don't you?"

"He's a boy I knew back home," I said hastily.

"Him?" she asked, pointing rudely at Charles. "From Abilene? You've got to be kidding!" Her eyes swept over my features with grudging admiration. "You've changed, friend." An arm waved in airy dismissal. "Have yourself a time. The key's under the mat."

And that's how I came to find myself dining in spendor in the Lotus Room of the fabulous Fairmont Hotel with my erudite and charming companion, Charles Christian.

He ordered champagne, blue points on the half shell and other delicacies, before he reached across the table for my hand. "Marly, I'm glad I found you! You're looking at a guy who is totally forsaken, lonely, and without human companionship. You couldn't have been more heaven-sent into my drab life."

He sounded so bereft that I laughed. "Oh, come now! You must have friends—or did you simply crash that party?"

"That's my pad," he said indifferently. "All the guests were the crashers. I don't know any of them."

"Oh, Charles—don't you even know my friend, BJ? She said we were invited."

"In a general sort of way," he admitted. "You let the word get around. But let's talk about you, darling. What brought you west?"

I told him about my assignment. He listened to the end, then emitted a whistle. "Regent, huh? I've heard the name from the misty past, and there's something else, too—an old castle—diminishing funds—" He pressed his folded hands against his head in concentration. "Some kind of mystery—what was it?"

"I have no idea," I said apprehensively, watching his face. "I was told that Mrs. Regent is something of a recluse and in financial straits, but the salary is good—even excellent by Midwest standards."

"And you left Kansas City to bury yourself somewhere in the wilderness with an old lady in an old house? You must be desperate for money, Marly. Can I help you out temporarily?"

"No, no!" I said hastily. "Besides, I'm not desperate, Charles. I thought it sounded like an interesting case, that's all. Do you realize I've never seen the ocean, except for the marine view from your apartment?"

"Then we'll grab a cab and go look at it," he said happily. "We'll walk on the beach barefoot and I'll collect that kiss you promised me once long ago." We both laughed merrily.

In the cab, he held my hand. "My father sent me out here to open a West Coast branch for our firm," he explained while I gazed at the steep hills and cringed at the rapid descent to the Embarcadero. "It's not exactly a friendly place, though. I haven't had a date in six months—until tonight."

"But you got along very well in England, didn't you? It isn't like you to be shy, Charles."

He hugged me to him affectionately. "If only you were staying in the city! Look, if it's work you want, we're hiring at the office. Can you type or do books or shorthand—anything like that?"

I shook my head. "No. And besides, I've already promised Mrs. Regent. I'm really looking forward to the assignment. I think it might be interesting. Since my parents and Matt died, I've sort of been a member of the floating population. I want to belong to someone again."

"You poor kid! How about belonging to me?"

I didn't dignify the suggestion by a reply simply because Charles hadn't meant it seriously. We left the cab at Seal Rock and walked down the dunes to the deserted beach. There, because he seemed to expect it, I stripped off my hose and sandals, and he did the same. We romped along the wet sand hand in hand— he in his dark business suit and I in my flame chiffon party gown—and when we came to the edge of the surf he lifted my face and kissed me gently.

"That's for being such a dear, sweet girl," he said huskily before claiming my lips again. This time, we drew apart, both of us breathless and shaking. "I could fall for you, Marly—I really could!" There was a note of wonder in his voice. "When are you leaving?"

"Tomorrow," I said wistfully. For I, too, would have liked to know Charles better now that we had been reunited by fate. "I'm to call a Mr. Davidson in the morning and he is to drive me down to Big Sur. Do you know where that is?"

"It's a long way to be driving with a stranger," he said protectively. "See here, my girl, let me take you. Who's this Davidson, anyway?"

"I don't know exactly," I said, pleased at his concern for me. "He seems to be about the only friend

Mrs. Regent has—at least it was under his auspices that I was engaged to care for her."

"Manages her affairs, does he? Something like that?" There was a tinge of jealousy in the next question, I thought. "How old is he?"

He drew my arm through his as we walked along. At the edge of the dark horizon, the waters of the ocean raged ceaselessly. I felt the excitement of its power as the spray stung my face. "I don't know, Charles. I don't know much of anything, except that I'll no longer be a nonentity once I'm established at Regent Manor. That's what they call it. Doesn't it sound delightful?"

"I don't like it," he said moodily, refusing to share my optimism. "It doesn't sound—safe. I mean, a kid like you knocking about in this way."

"I've been knocking about alone for a long time now," I said, unperturbed.

His fingers closed over my hand. "Nevertheless, I'm driving you down tomorrow. I'm going to see first-hand what you've let yourself in for. And if it isn't any good, I'll bring you right back with me."

He sounded very concerned and protective for such a carefree, rich, and spoiled young man.

CHAPTER 2

I was fitfully awake on the narrow cot in BJ's basement most of the night. Night noises roused me into full wakefulness from time to time, and I imagined that I could hear the rats gnawing along the partitions. Occasionally, a foghorn blew mournfully, sending chills up and down my spine.

In her own corner under the shelves, BJ slept peacefully on a cot as crude as mine. I couldn't reconcile myself to her acceptance of all this when, considering her background at home, she had had "everything," according to Kansas standards. Mr. Barnett was a banker in Abilene, and it was an established fact that bankers always occupied the nicest houses in the small towns where they lived. The Barnett home was no exception. Roomy and squarely comfortable, it boasted a wide screened porch which was, in summer, the scene of BJ's lesser triumphs of popularity. Whenever I walked by in the evenings, music blared and I could see couples dancing and hear their laughter and the clink of ice in tall glasses. And BJ was "an only child," which meant in Abilene parlance that she was pampered, popular, spoiled, and sought after. To leave all that for this?

When the first faint streaks of dawn bore through the slits of the windows, I remembered what BJ had said last night about the shower, and, taking a towel from the rack, I set out into the gloomy basement to have an invigorating bath. It wasn't such a bad place, the bathroom, after I had scrubbed the tub and filled it with hot, soapy water. I felt quite human again when I had soaked luxuriously and was back in the cellar room where my friend still slept.

She roused herself while I was repacking and said curiously, "You're not leaving, are you?"

"Didn't I tell you last night that I'm due to report for duty today?"

"Well, for Pete's sake, wait till I rustle around and make us some coffee!" She threw on a paint-stained smock that had seen better days and rummaged on the shelves for a half-jar of instant coffee and a dented aluminum pan, filling the latter and putting it on the gas plate. "How'd you get along last night with What's-his-name? I mean, wasn't he our host, or did I take you to the wrong blast?"

I poured juice from a can and said evasively, "His name is Charles Christian, BJ, and I happened to have known him in Kansas City."

"Why, you sly owl! You mean, you followed him out here to SF?"

It was no use, I thought, trying to convince BJ of anything. She and I had nothing in common, and although she had written rather frantically for me to come and be her guest for as long as I liked, I knew that this short visit had done nothing to bridge the chasm between a small town's distinction of the farmer's daughter and the banker's daughter. I sat down on the wobbly cot and cradled the mug of lukewarm coffee in my hands.

"BJ, I thought I made it clear in my letter that I'm out here on a case."

"Case for matrimony, I hope." She grinned. "Oh,

I saw him smoothing in on you last night. Did he take you anywhere decent?"

"Charles," I said with dignity, "took me to the Fairmont."

"Ha!" She took a quick sip of the cool orange juice and a calculating light came into her dark eyes. "Money, huh? I must write home and ask Daddy for his credentials. What did you say his last name is?"

My eyes moved along the dingy surroundings in dismay. "Why," I asked icily, "would you want to do a thing like that? If you aren't contented here, can't you paint just as well at home? You have every comfort there."

"What?" she asked, aghast. "And end up an old maid like Mona Lyle and Kate Palmer?" She leaned forward intently. "Listen—every eligible male in that town has either married or gone elsewhere." She began to pace the floor restlessly. "I don't care anything about painting. I'm husband-hunting—it's as simple as that. And if your Charles is up for grabs, watch my smoke!"

"*I* don't feel like an old maid," I said mildly. "If I'd had a home like yours—"

She interrupted with an exclamation of disgust: "Smother-love! I had to get away. No matter if they did cut my allowance to the bone! I keep writing back how successful I am, and all that rot, to keep them off my back. And you, my dear and lovable house guest, have brought me the first big break I've had since I came here three years ago. This town is overpopulated with gals looking for husbands! Now that Charles—what's his last name again?"

I busied myself at the gas jet, heating more coffee and wondering how I could keep Charles from her eager grasp. For one thing, that kiss last night had been rather shattering and I didn't want BJ spoiling its aftermath. For another, I couldn't imagine how Charles would regard the squalor of this ugly place. With that in mind, I had asked him to call me this morning when he was ready to start and assured him that I'd rather meet him in the garage to save time. Now the phone rang and saved me from being obliged to reply. BJ answered it, and turned to me with that smug cat's smile of hers.

"It's Charles. He says he's ready to leave." She put her hands on her hips. "Is *he* your 'patient'?"

"He's driving me down," I said shortly. "Thanks for having me, BJ. I'll keep in touch."

Charles looked smashing in a white turtle-neck shirt and double-breasted navy blazer that made his hair even fairer and his wide smile whiter. He kissed my chin as he took my bags, and when they were neatly stowed in the trunk of the same bullet-car I'd known in Kansas City, he caught me in his arms and said joyously, "Hello, you lovely you! Hop in, darling, and we'll have breakfast on the way." When we were clear of the garage and out into the murky dawn, he said, "The sun'll be shining farther down." Then, in a lower tone, "I didn't sleep much last night, thinking about you."

The city was barely beginning to stir—a few milk trucks and bread deliveries, a sleepy tourist or two with Ohio and Illinois license tags and children in the back blinking tiredly. Charles kept on talking, pointing out to me the fine old homes along the Panhandle, from which, he said, Golden Gate Park had grown.

"A Scotsman named John MacLaren planted the dunes and made them into this beauty spot," he said. "And made liars of the scoffers who said that nothing would grow in the sand. Look over there, darling, at that funny old house with the gables. Isn't it something else? You know, when I get this office set up I think I'll go abroad again and study architecture." He glanced at me obliquely, smiling. "You're awfully quiet this morning. Don't you think you'd like being married to an architect?"

"You aren't marrying anyone for a long time yet," I scoffed. "But I like your idea for building."

"Think of it!" he said with growing enthusiasm. "Think of going back to the Midwest and introducing every type of home—like those over there. Can't you see them lining the streets of your home town?"

The idea was so brash that I couldn't help laughing. Charles didn't know the square, strong, comfortable homes of Abilene as I did. They were built to withstand the rigors of cyclone and tornado, to keep their occupants safe and warm in winter and cool in the blazing heat and wind of summer.

"You're marvelous," I said, smiling back at him. "I shouldn't wonder if a bright young man like you didn't set the world on fire."

We reached the Great Highway just as a sickly sun struggled through the fog to herald the new day. Lacy froth teased the sands and receded again while sandpipers left their tiny tracks in the wet. Gulls screamed overhead, gliding and dipping as they watched for fish below. And in another few miles, the sky was clear and blue and the rising sun a fiery orb.

"Breakfast," Charles said, pulling into a quaint little inn perched on a cliff. "I could eat a horse. How about you?"

"I'll settle for a rasher of bacon, and an egg. Where I come from, we don't eat horses."

Our table overlooked the sea, smashing against the rocks far below, and as I watched, fascinated, Charles said, "I'm glad you let me come along today. I want to be with you as long as I can."

All at once, it occurred to me that I wouldn't be having breakfast if it were not for him. I had seven dollars and a few cents in my purse. With sincere affection, I said warmly, "This is so good of you, Charles. What would I have done without you?"

"You mean you like me better than old Papa Davidson?" he joked. "Maybe if I hang around I'll be able to nudge him out of the picture. Kidding aside," he said when our tantalizing plates had been placed before us by a perky mini-skirted waitress, "you've given me a whole new horizon, showing up so unexpectedly last night. A new lease on life."

"How so?" I asked curiously. "You didn't look too unhappy in that mob."

"Strangers! Not a friendly face in sight. Until that particular face smiled at me."

"And you didn't even remember my name," I chided. "I could see that you'd been longing for a glimpse of me and my smile."

"Cut it out," he said, stuffing a large piece of ham in his mouth.

It wasn't that Charles was insincere, I thought, watching him eat with such apparent enjoyment. In fact, he ardently believed whatever he said at the moment, and he was a delightful boy. But just a boy. Somehow, in his background of adoration and riches and travel, he had neglected to grow up. And I—I had grown up too fast, or perhaps grown old too soon. But at least he was making the trip to Regent Manor far more pleasant and my own anxiety less. For who could yield to anxiety with the sun shining and all the birds vying with one another in song?

The pert waitress brought more coffee and hovered about with a look of embarrassment before she said, "Pardon me, but are you two just married? I have a bet with the fry cook that you are."

Charles gave her his slow grin that reached his blue eyes and made him so charming. "You go collect your wager then," he said, giving me a conspiratorial wink. "We're on our honeymoon."

When she had scurried away, I said, "Charles, you nut!"

"You don't have much confidence in me, do you?" he asked, gulping his coffee with much enjoyment. The expression in his eyes was rather strange now. "Perhaps I'll have an opportunity to prove myself to you when we get to the haunted castle in Big Sur."

"Doing what?" I laughed to take the edge off the moment. "Jousting, perhaps, or dueling?"

"I'd feel a lot easier," he said gloomily, "if you'd promise to call me in the city—that is, if anything goes wrong, or you don't like the setup." He scribbled both phones on a card and held it out to me. I tucked it carefully in my purse, moved by his care of me. Even if I knew that Charles Christian could forget me as easily as he had before, I was touched by his gesture.

We started out again in the bullet-car. Charles drove well, but fast, except when we came to a scenic view or historical marker. Then he would pull over and listen to my exclamations of pleasure, explaining the historical significance with patient care, as though he had passed this way many times before.

"You've made quite a study of California lore," I said with admiration. "What a good guide you are. I can almost see the brown-robed missionaries trudging along these hills with their donkey packs and weary followers. What has happened to all their missions?"

"I'll show you Santa Clara," he offered, pleased at my appreciation. "But I think the remarkable thing was the first town they established, San Jose. In the seventeen seventies, when the missions and presidios were flourishing, they were faced with another problem—that of sustenance. The Santa Clara valley was fertile—still is—but it needed a colony to produce foodstuffs." He flashed me a smile. "Don't let me bore you with my pedagogery."

"You're not boring me in the least."

"All right then—these good and holy blokes christened their first pueblo—a small community consisting of nine soldiers and five settlers, who were provided with land, supplies, horses, cattle, and sheep. Then, in effect, the missionaries said, 'Get to it,' and gave them a blessing."

"And was the venture successful?"

"I'll let you judge for yourself when we get to San Jose," he said. "We'll see the mission and have lunch there."

"I couldn't," I protested. "Let's wait until we are farther on our way."

We crossed green and fertile valleys, wound through the hills, and, after a lingering inspection of the mission and the sprawling agricultural town, moved along at a good clip toward the coastal road. Every view was breath-taking, with throbbing blue ocean and calm blue sky. Yellow mustard and blue lupine and wild poppies scattered their color on the hills. The smell of cauliflower, leek, and lettuce testified to the industry of the farmers. "Ranchers" Charles said they were called, not "farmers."

The afternoon was well along by the time we reached Monterey. We stopped and prowled for a bit along Fisherman's Wharf, munching shrimp in paper cups as we strolled. Trawlers and sailboats dotted the waters, some docked and some setting out for the catch. Over the graying horizon, several dark clouds loomed, no bigger than a man's hand, but by the time we had reached the car again, raindrops thudded against the windshield.

"I'm tired and stiff," Charles complained. "Let's stop for a long, relaxing dinner in Carmel and make it a farewell party."

I had much rather have continued on our way. My curiosity about my new "home" was taking precedence again over the pleasures of the trip. But Charles would have the long drive back to the city tonight, and I did not have the heart to refuse him.

It was raining hard by the time we cruised the main thoroughfare for a quick glimpse of the quaint and sleepy little village and stopped before the Pine Inn. While I freshened up in the ladies' lounge, Charles took the car to be gassed and checked. When he rejoined me, he was dripping wet, but rubbing his hands together in anticipation of dinner and a rest.

We had our drinks before a small fire in an old-fashioned grate. The bar was nearly deserted, and we began to speculate on how to find Regent Manor. The bartender, polishing glasses, must have overheard, because he gave minute directions, then asked, "What are you going there for? They won't let you past the gates."

"Why not?" Charles countered.

"Mrs. Regent don't care to see anyone." He touched his temple warily with one blunt finger. "She's gone a little daffy, I hear."

"Oh, great!" Charles muttered under his breath. "You're going to be nursemaid to a lunatic."

Ignoring him, I asked the bartender, "What about tradespeople? Surely they must be admitted?"

He shook his head solemnly, glad to be the harbinger of bad news. "Nobody gets in except by appointment—not even her doctor. As for supplies, old Jock comes to town once a week with a list, and that's the last you see of *him*. He's as cagey as the next one, too, never peeps one-two-three. If you ask me, that old castle is full of creeps."

Doubly curious now, I began to question him rather mercilessly. How many occupied the premises? He didn't know. How was Mrs. Regent's health? He didn't know. Having divulged the full extent of his information, the bartender seemed to have lost interest. Other customers were claiming his attention now, and Charles leaned toward me to whisper, "Come back to the city with me, Marly. This is not your dish of tea."

"No, I'm going all the way with it," I said stubbornly. Then I added, "But I am glad you're available, Charles. Somehow, I'm less frightened having you along." Then a thought struck me that left me weak! "Oh, Charles, I forgot to call Mr. Davidson! How could I have done such a thing? He's probably waited all day for my call. He might even assume that I've changed my mind and not come at all."

"April Fool's Day." Charles grinned. "Forget it! You can call him when you get to the house of horrors. Let's go in to dinner."

The dining room was resplendent with antiques, which I must pause to admire and exclaim over, with pewter mugs and pitchers, old sideboards, and gleaming candelabra. We were shown to a table overlooking the street, where we could revel in the warmth and light while the rain beat against the windows with increasing fury.

"I'm going to take you inside and wait with you," Charles said intensely, "while you get your bearings. Then, if everything isn't to your liking, I'll take you back with me."

"The storm is getting on your nerves," I said gently, "but I do appreciate your kindness. What worries me more than anything is your having to drive all the way back in this."

"The roads will be deserted," he said easily. "But this thing with you is different."

I tried to get him back on the subject of California history, but without success. Finally, with a restrained note of mutual relief, we tackled our delicious and well-served dinner. This restored us both to good humor and a spirit of anticipation. I could harly wait to be on our way and my feet were literally dancing with impatience under the table while Charles prolonged his coffee by ordering after-dinner cordials.

"It's only thirty miles or so," he said comfortably, "and only seven o'clock. We'll have plenty of time to get there before bedtime."

I didn't tell him that it would be my duty to prepare Mrs. Regent for her night's rest and that often elderly patients are disagreeably hard to get off to sleep. They wanted warm milk, which must be heated to an exact temperature. Sometimes they remained garrulous for hours, loath to be left alone in the dark. And I was tired from my sleepless night and the excitement of this day. But Charles was impervious to all that and continued to chat amiably. I felt that I had come to know him considerably better during this day and, to me, he had assumed the identity of a pleasant little boy who behaved remarkably well unless he was crossed. I didn't wish to cross him, so I waited. Time passed in leaden minutes. Charles wanted to watch the storm breaking over the ocean at the foot of Ocean Avenue. The view was spectacular and rendered us both silent for some time. Afterward we plowed our way through the downpour along the slippery curves.

The first sketch of Regent Manor was so fleeting that Charles noticed it not at all as it dipped from sight. Instinctively, though, I knew that this was it! I strained my eyes for the next glimpse of it, and when it came, high above, I gasped with awe and cried, "Oh, Charles!"

"Can't look," he said tersely, "without wrecking us both. Tell me how it looks. Horrible?"

"Oh, no," I denied. "It's magnificent, with towers and wings and cupolas—and an immense tower somewhere behind overlooking everything. Could it be a watchtower? But you can't drive up there, Charles. It's on a rocky cliff—there's no road. We'll have to run for it through the rain."

"Dark, is it?"

"There's a light in every window," I said joyously. "Oh, it looks so majestic—and so very friendly! Do take a look, Charles."

"Great Scott!" he breathed reverently.

CHAPTER 3

We stood under the three arches of the veranda, drenched, as I pulled the bell and heard it reverberate through the house. I could not see through the wide double doors of heavy oak, but there were reassuring sounds from within, voices and footsteps coming closer.

A bolt slid across the wood with a rasping sound, then a key turned in the lock and a rich, comfortable voice asked, "Yes? Who is it?" before opening the door a crack.

I saw a plump, rosy-cheeked woman with snapping brown eyes. Her hair was pulled straight back to a knot that was so tight it made her eyes slant. Charles stepped forward while I was regarding her and trying to decide whether she was friendly or rigidly formal. She was wearing a stiffly starched white apron, so I took her to be a servant.

"I have brought the nurse," Charles said manfully. "Miss Marly Carewe."

"Miss Carewe?" she repeated. "But how did you get in the gates?"

"Simple," Charles said belligerently, showing his muddy hands. "We were obliged to crawl over. Weren't you expecting Miss Carewe?"

She caught my eye then, and after a quick scrutiny pulled the door wider and allowed us to enter. "Well, yes, but I had almost given you up in this storm." She held out a hand to me, ignoring Charles. "I'm Mrs. Livingston, the housekeeper. We were informed that Michael was driving you down, but when he called —well, I gave it up then." She turned to Charles accusingly, and I was free to observe my surroundings. "You shouldn't have crawled over the gates," she scolded. "Look at you—and you've torn your trousers. Come with me to the washroom under the stairs."

Charles followed her obediently and I stared up the massive stairway of carved walnut, hoping to see the other occupants of the house. At first, I thought it was a child peering down over the balustrade; then I saw that she was a young girl. I smiled up at her, but she continued to regard me without expression. Her sorrel hair hung over her shoulders from a part in the middle and the face was heart-shaped and very pretty, I thought. I was about to identify myself when Mrs. Livingston returned and, following my eyes, gave an involuntary exclamation.

"Annette!" she said loudly. "Go back to your room, you hear? And stay there!" I had another bold scrutiny from those lively brown eyes before she said, "Come in to the fire, Miss Carewe. You're all wet."

I had an overwhelming impression of dark, elegant furnishings, rugs and draperies, but the fire burning brightly under a wide marble mantel was irresistible. I moved to it and stood rubbing my hands and shivering slightly.

Mrs. Livingston spoke from behind me. "You shouldn't have forced the gates, and you should have had Michael bring you." She brought a log for the fire and poked it in obvious annoyance. "You see, he meant to interview you first for your—suitability."

I felt my own irritation rise to meet hers. I was wet and bedraggled and weary, and I didn't like her display of authority. "I should think," I said, "that Mrs. Regent might better be the judge of that! As for Mr. Davidson, he relied on the judgment of an old friend of his father's for my credentials—Dr. Burley."

"Ah, well," she retorted, "things have changed considerably since then, as things have a way of doing here. However, stay the night and Mrs. Regent will see you in the morning."

Had not Charles appeared just then, I'm afraid I might have refused the reluctant invitation. But Charles had been so sure that I was getting into a hornet's nest that I wouldn't give him the satisfaction. Besides, I was curious about this place, and about my patient. Why did Mr. Davidson have the last word? And why was it a crime to climb over the gates when there was no one around to admit us?

"You'll be all right?" Charles said in an undertone. I thought he seemed reassured at the cheerful aspect of the premises.

"Well," I said with false heartiness, "I do thank you so much for bringing me down." I put out my hand in a gesture of dismissal. Mrs. Livingston was looking on all this with her knowing eyes. Poor Charles did look a bit shabby from the mud and wet, I thought, and I wished that she would ask him to stay overnight, or at least long enough to have something hot and dry off a bit. But she seemed as anxious for his departure as I.

"Good night," said Charles with admirable poise, and turning to Mrs. Livingston, he repeated, "Good night."

I blessed him silently as he followed the housekeeper to the door and left without any argument. Evidently he was satisfied.

But I was not. When Mrs. Livingston returned, I began, "Now, as far as Mr. Davidson is concerned—"

"No more discussion tonight," she interrupted spunkily. "You'll want a hot bath and your warm bed." She picked up one of my bags and nodded toward the other. "Come, follow me."

I felt my anger dissipate entirely at her mention of bath and bed. I was so tired that my legs felt like rubber on the stairs. Again, I had a vague impression of soft carpets, lovely paintings, beauty and order as we reached the upper hall. This was no creepy castle with cobwebs hanging from the walls and queer wailings from the attic. This was a spacious and luxurious home, perfectly kept and obviously cherished. I found myself hoping ardently that I could stay. Given time, I thought I could win Mrs. Livingston, Mr. Davidson, my patient, and anyone else who showed antipathy. I began to regret that we had scaled the gates and made my start on the wrong foot in this blissful haven.

A small fire burned in the grate of my sitting room. Fresh flowers graced the marble-top table beside a deep chair. Under a great window, draped in soft green velvet and lined in magenta, a loveseat of the same green was scattered with accent cushions. Before it, on a low bowlegged coffee table, was a bowl of fruit and a tea tray. The room was paneled halfway up in the same green, with the upper half of the walls papered brightly in magenta. There were pictures and vases and bowls about, and another comfortable chair with a pile of books beside it. The room looked welcoming, gracious and beautiful.

Mrs. Livingston sailed through it without a glance and flung open the door to my bedroom. Here, the magenta had been carried for the sake of color harmony, but only in small accents. The rest was a soft cream, and beyond I could see that marvel of marvels, a tiled, gleaming bathroom.

Mrs. Livingston put my bag down and smiled at me. It transformed her face completely, touching the eyes and lilting the mouth beguilingly.

"Do you like it?" she asked hospitably. My expression must have told her, because she went on: "The door from your sitting room connects with Mrs. Regent's suite. She will not wish to be disturbed until after she rings for breakfast and sends for you. That will be about nine o'clock, so make sure you're ready by that time." She smiled again, more formally, and bade me good night.

I stood speechless in the middle of the bedroom, looking with longing first at the bed, then at the glistening bathroom. What a place and what a salary! *Oh, dear God, please let them like me!*

After I had bathed in lavender-scented soap and unpacked to put on my prettiest negligee, I felt a part of all the wondrous affluence. I sat for a while before the fire, which was rapidly dying to embers. Which way, I wondered, did my rooms face? I pulled back the silky curtains and looked out into the rain. Oblongs of light still came from the downstairs windows, and I thought I must be at the far side of the main portico. Yes, surely, that was it, for Mrs. Regent's suite would look directly down upon the main entrance and the gates beyond. Had she seen our disreputable arrival? I wondered. What could she have thought of a man and woman running hand in hand through the downpour? That we were intruders, no doubt.

I poured a cup of tea and pondered my own situation. If I were not hired, I would be faced with the expense of returning to Kansas City, asking for my job back at St. Joseph's and confronting Dr. Burley with my failure. Even the hot tea and tiny sandwiches did not dispel the gloom of such a prospect. Otherwise, I would have to borrow money from Charles and seek employment at some San Francisco hospital. After this, I could never go back to BJ's hovel. In fact, I wanted to stay right here forever!

I had just removed my negligee and turned back the fat comforters on the inviting bed when I heard a faint scratching like that of a small animal. It startled me, and I stopped still, listening. It came again, from the direction of the sitting room. I went in there and switched on a table light. Then it came again—a hoarse little mewing sound. Someone was in the hall!

I pulled back the bolt on the door and, as the sound came again, I opened it cautiously.

On the floor, huddled forlornly, was the young girl I had seen earlier from the stair. She was in a thin nightgown and shivering pitifully. Her big blue eyes looked up at me fearfully. What was it the housekeeper had called her? Annette? I reached down to pull her to her feet.

"Annette," I said very gently, "what is the matter? Come inside, dear, to the fire."

She was like a frightened kitten, letting me lead her to a chair and clinging to me with childish trust. I could see now that she was older than I had first thought—perhaps fifteen or so—and there was a curious blankness in the beautiful face. "Are you afraid, darling, of the storm?"

She nodded, the great blank stare never leaving my face. This poor child was retarded, I thought, and terribly afraid. Talking in the same low voice, I poured her a cup of tea and sat on the arm of the chair, holding it while she drank. I brought the remainder of the sandwiches, and she fell upon them greedily, pushing the bread into her mouth until it was full, choking when she tried to swallow. I gave her another drink of tea to wash down the food and thought, *Dear Heaven, this poor child is half-starved!*

When she had devoured a peach and several figs from the fruit bowl, she leaned back with a sigh of contentment and put her legs under her.

"Where do you sleep?" I asked. "Shall I take you back to your room?"

"No!" She sounded like a naughty child. "I want to stay with you!" She jumped to her feet and ran to the loveseat. I noticed what lovely slim legs she had and how gracefully shaped were the bare feet. She curled up there, like a kitten, and said, "I won't be a bother."

This was a peculiar situation in which to find myself on my first night in a strange house. As I hesitated, her eyes begged me mutely. "All right, then, I'll find you some blankets," I said reluctantly.

"And I can watch the little men in the fire?"

I found the blankets on the closet shelf and covered her well. "You must try to go to sleep," I said. "The storm is nearly over, and tomorrow the sun will shine."

"Oh, see the little men dancing!" She pointed to the last flame licking the ashes. "I like you," she babbled. "How did you know my name? I wish I had a fire. Do you like me?"

"Very much," I assured her with pity in my heart. "You're a lovely girl, and we shall be friends."

"Friends?" She pondered the word as though it were unfamiliar. "Is—Michael—my friend?" There was the faintest tinge of mistrust in the query.

"I don't know Michael," I said soothingly. "But you and I are friends."

She clutched at my hand with her long, slim fingers. "Stay with me," she implored. I saw the dainty yawn, and the weariness that would soon bear her off to slumber. I sat quietly until her breathing was regular, then I turned out the light and went to bed.

When I awoke the next morning, Annette was gone. There was only the huddle of blankets to give evidence that she had visited my rooms at all. I gathered them up hastily and, folding them, put them back on the closet shelf.

I was fully dressed when I heard a faint tinkle, which I presumed to be Mrs. Regent's bell. It was exactly nine o'clock. I waited ten or fifteen minutes, looking down on the terrace where the sun was drying off the bricks and emanating little tufts of moisture. There was a discreet knock on my door.

The woman who stood there must be at least thirty, dark and sallow, with something familiar about her mouth and bone structure.

"I'm Vivian, Mrs. Livingston's daughter," she announced almost belligerently. There was a furtive look in the slitted dark eyes which I did not like at all, even though I was inclined to be attracted to her cheery mother. "Mrs. Regent wants you now."

I felt a little like the second upstairs maid at the sound of the summons. Vivian might have phrased it differently, but looking at her run-down shoes and slatternly appearance, I thought that she cared little for manners. Maybe she didn't know any better, although her mother seemed to have a rather forceful comeliness about her. At least, she had been quite nice when she said good night.

Mrs. Regent's sitting room opened from the hall, as well as from my room, I saw. It was in shades of blue and lavender, somewhat larger than mine, and there was an alcove where a small writing desk stood. The windows were open to the sun and fresh morning air, and I noticed a balcony through the French doors.

She was sitting up in bed, and almost at once, I saw

why she preferred shades of blue in her decor. Her eyes were a dazzling blue, her white hair piled high in an elaborate coiffure, her bedjacket of the most delicate embroidered silk. She looked to be in her middle sixties, and her creamy smooth skin testified to exceptionally good health although the fingers on her cup were knotted with arthritis.

She scrutinized me keenly as she asked me to sit down.

"You'll find your own breakfast on the table over there, Miss Carewe," she said graciously. "I hope you will not think us too informal, but I like to have company after the long night. Your lunch you may have anywhere you like—perhaps a picnic on the terrace on such a beautiful day as this?" I murmured something in assent, and she continued talking to put me at my ease. "I hope you had a good sleep, my dear. If not, you are free to nap, as I do in the afternoon. There is one strict house rule, though, which prevails in good weather or foul. Cocktails at five, even when we are alone, and dinner at half-past seven."

I uncovered the silver tray, thoroughly enjoying this delightful woman and her chatter. There was orange juice in a silver ice container, bacon and eggs, and tiny hot rolls with jam. I was truly hungry, and Mrs. Regent sipped her coffee while I ate, her magnificent eyes coming to me again and again.

"Vivian is my personal maid," she said, "and is somewhat jealous of her position. So in order not to hurt her rather sensitive feelings, we'll continue as we are for the present. She tends to my bath, dresses me for dinner, and"—she lifted her hands eloquently—"is most devoted, if somewhat glum." She smiled. "I say this, not in criticism, but so that you will understand and overlook her idiosyncrasies. Mrs. Livingston, the housekeeper, is her mother."

"I met her last night," I said. "She seemed very—pleasant."

"Jock is her husband. I brought them all with me from Scotland, although Mrs. Livingston isn't a Scot. They looked after me over there when I was on tour, even going to England and France with me. Then, when I had my accident— You knew that I broke my back in a fall from a horse?"

"Yes," I said. "Dr. Burley told me. In Spain, wasn't it?"

"I was laid up for months and months," she went on, but without self-pity. "So I sent for my faithful friends, and they agreed to break up their own home to come here with me. Vivian was only a child then."

I willed her to go on, hoping that she would say something about my elfin visitor of the night, Annette. "My only daughter, Sylvia, had just been married at the time and was living in England, you see. Her husband died a few years later and"—for the first time, she showed emotion—"dear Sylvia was on her way to me when she became ill and died, too, in New York."

"How terribly sad!" I said with genuine sympathy.

After a moment, she regained control and said mistily, "I think that is one reason I am going to enjoy having you here so much, Miss Carewe—Marly, if I may? You see, Sylvia and I were very companionable. We enjoyed music, and reading together. And after Mr. Regent's death, she was my constant companion until her marriage."

"I'm sure I shall enjoy your company, too, Mrs. Regent," I said quickly. Apparently, there was no question in my patient's mind about my staying on. But she hardly needed a nurse, I thought. She was alert, beautifully groomed, and in no apparent pain. Why did she want me, unless as a companion? However, I didn't feel this was quite the time to ask misleading questions. She might think me discontent with my situation while, actually, quite the opposite was true. I really felt that I could be happy in this magnificent home and in the company of this charming woman.

"The rest of the household is under the dominion of Mrs. Livingston and Jock," she said. "The maids are Rose and Kate, sisters. They are agreeable girls, and quite orderly. They live in, as do the others. There is an excellent cook in the kitchen, Delphia, and Jock brings in outside men for the seasonal gardening and heavy house-cleaning. So you see, we're quite a menage—and if you want anything, you have only to ask for it. Some of the rooms are closed off for convenience' sake, but you are free to go whereever you like." Her voice dropped to a wistful tone. "There is a music room in the west wing that I'd like to show you myself sometime. I rarely go there any more, of course, but it was once the center of activity in this house."

"I'm sure it must be lovely," I said in the pause. "All that I've seen here is—beautiful."

Her eyes narrowed slightly as they bore into mine. "You're sure you won't be lonely here? Mrs. Livingston discourages outside social activity for her own reasons—perhaps, for my sake—I don't know. At any rate, we lead sedentary lives here, but we get along very well together. I am more or less helpless, as you see, and since most of my old friends in the vicinity are gone elsewhere, or have died, I never entertain any more." Her face twinkled in a smile that I was to know well in days to come. "However, with a young lady in the house once more, I might be persuaded to do so sometime in the future."

I smiled back at her and said, "I'm sure that I shall

be quite happy with things as they are, Mrs. Regent. But you must tell me my duties, or I cannot be content to accept such a generous salary."

"Oh," she said airily, "flower arranging—things like that. Reading together and, of course, the music. I have an extensive library of recordings downstairs, some of them my own. I like to listen to them and re-live the occasions of their rendition."

"I heard that you were a concert pianist, and very famous," I murmured, pouring more coffee for her and for myself.

Her laugh was like the tinkle of a spring falling over rocks. "That is putting it mildly. I was the 'toast of the Continent,' as one nice critic put it." She looked at her gnarled hands. "It would seem that I could have, at least, kept my fingers," she added without any trace of bitterness. "And now, my dear, if you've finished your breakfast, why don't you run along and let Vivian in to help me with my morning ablutions? I'm running a little late this morning, due to this very pleasant chat, and she will be impatient."

"I've enjoyed it, too," I said, rising and starting for the door. "If there is anything *I* can do for you—?"

"Oh yes, there is! Letters! I still carry on a heavy correspondence with friends abroad. Do you write a legible hand?"

"Yes, I do," I said without false modesty. "Whenever you want me, Mrs. Regent."

"Well, not today. So do go enjoy yourself this first day and I'll see you at five downstairs in the library. We'll have a festive evening of music, shall we?"

It was not until I had nearly fallen over Vivian in the hall that I realized the sulky maid had been listening outside the door for some time.

And there was something else, too. Mrs. Regent had not said one word about Annette.

CHAPTER 4

My first week at Regent Manor passed without incident.

I made many discoveries. The castle was set upon solid rock that descended some sixty feet down to the sea below, where the cliffs were black with the constant battle of the water and an accumulation of moss and seaweed. Since my rooms were at the front of the house, I could not hear the noisy roar of the waves, but on the back terrace on a windy day, it was almost deafening. The size of the mansion staggered the imagination. I could see that there must be at least fifty or more rooms, including, of course, the servants' quarters, which looked from the outside to be quite spacious and comfortable on the slant under the eaves at the back. From the front, the facade rose straight and true to the third floor. I guessed that Mrs. Regent's music salon was directly above her own second-floor suite.

After that first evening with Mrs. Regent, I felt that we were unusually compatible. We had shared several jokes and expressions that gave us amusement. She was an intrepid woman who never complained, although I had seen her wince more than once when she thought herself unobserved.

I asked her that first night if I might give her an aspirin or Nembutol, but she shook her head, saying,

"I take nothing, my dear. I like to rely on faith alone."

Often I wondered why I was at Regent Manor. My duties, although pleasant, had nothing to do with the care of my "patient." Vivian bathed and dressed her, tended the carefully groomed hair and was usually near her mistress' rooms when not in actual attendance. Mrs. Livingston, more talkative than her sullen daughter, explained that it embarrassed Mrs. Regent to have anyone but Vivian see her bodily defects.

"Vivian's used to her, having been only a child when we came here. She's devoted to the madam, and very possessive."

I took the hint and stayed out of the way unless summoned by Mrs. Regent. When this occurred above-stairs, I always felt that Vivian resented the intrusion. At cocktails and dinnertime, however, Vivian made herself scarce, and I had Mrs. Regent all to myself.

Dinner was a formal and dignified affair, with either Rose or Kate waiting on us in the massive dining room, where we sat at one end of the banquet-size table. There was always music piped in softly from the Stereo, and flowers and beautiful appointments, and Mrs. Regent's endless reminiscences of days gone by. I was content to listen, picturing to myself the triumphs of Europe's darling, the parties and fascinating salons, and fabulous names of great people. Just to be with Mrs. Regent was a tonic, and I could never have been bored with her scintillating conversation.

"When Mr. Regent came into my life," she might say, and go on into an interminable tale that held me spellbound until the end. She talked well, and she enjoyed opening the vistas of the past to me, her avid listener.

In the long, sunny afternoons I walked. I had discovered almost at once a lovely level beach far down the west side of the castle. I loved to lie there in the sun with my book and either read or dream as I looked at the ever-changing horizon. I had also discovered a little garden off the east wing, near a walled and bricked veranda. Here there were cushioned wicker chairs and couches and tables, to say nothing of flowering shrubs and every bright flower in a galaxy of bloom. Chrysanthemums, daisies, roses, philodendron, asters, violets, and marigolds changed seasons with other blossoms. The earth about them was always sweet and damp, and I loved to fill my basket with color, then take it to the pantry to make up beautiful bouquets for every room that was in use. Mrs. Regent particularly loved the delphinium.

I'd become rather well acquainted with Jock. He was forever puttering about the place, and he had a terse sort of wit and wisdom. He was craggy, sturdy, and short, and it was he who introduced me to the wonders of the east terrace and gardens where I usually had my lunch on sunny days. I never felt that I was intruding on Jock. Often we would talk, but there was companionship in our silences as well.

One foggy morning I came upon him overseeing a half-dozen workmen at the gates. They were raising the iron fence another three feet, enclosing the posts in cement.

"To insure against another such invasion as yours, Miss Marly," Jock said when he saw the mute question in my eyes. "The madam don't like trespassers, she don't. Viv tells me she was upset considerable when she heard how you got in that night, and with a stranger along, too."

"I wish she hadn't been bothered with that," I said disconsolately. "Besides, I don't see that it did any harm, since I was expected."

"But not with a stranger," he reminded me severely. "The mistress was unable to sleep that night, Viv tells me."

I resumed my stroll, the events of that first night returning to me. I could see that Mrs. Regent might be too proud to wish any of her former friends to see her crippled condition, but I was a nurse and engaged to care for her. Surely that might have made a difference. As for Charles, he need never see her. Had she, I wondered again, been at the window and seen us storming the gates? Perhaps it had frightened her, and I was sorry. But since she had never alluded to our strange entrance on that rainy night, I resolved not to do so, either.

And what about Annette? In her sleeplessness, had Mrs. Regent heard us in my rooms? I thought not; everything seemed to be as nearly soundproof as possible. But where *was* the child? I had asked no one, since I was not supposed to know of her existence. But I often wished that she might accompany me on my walks. She had appealed to the maternal instincts of my nature, and I could have told her stories, taught her many things. I looked back at the huge house, wondering which room had been hers. Who was she? And what had she been doing here? For I really believed that she must have been only an overnight guest. I remembered the harsh way in which Mrs. Livingston had spoken to her and how the lovely young face had disappeared obediently at the housekeeper's command.

I often wondered, too, about the girl's queer allusion to "Michael." That would be Mr. Davidson, who had not yet made an appearance at Regent Manor, although he was, supposedly, quite annoyed that I had not driven down with him. Wouldn't one suppose that he would be interested enough to come down and see the nurse that he had hired? Wouldn't he wonder if I were satisfactory to Mrs. Regent? Perhaps his interest had ended as suddenly as it had begun. Although Mrs. Livingston *had* spoken of him with familiarity. And Annette, too, had used his name as though he were a frequent visitor. The mystery of "Michael" and the mystery of Annette pricked my mind often. Did Mrs. Regent know of the girl's presence? I wondered. She was nearly helpless, and there might be many things that she did not know.

I thought of Charles, too, of course. Whatever romantic notions I had had of him in Kansas City had dissolved entirely. He was, I saw now, a fairly selfish person whose companionship was delightful, but never to be taken seriously. Jock had brought a letter from the village several days after my arrival.

"I think of you lolling in the lap of luxury, and am vastly reassured," he wrote. "Until you become accustomed, I presume you had rather I did not disrupt your life by calling—if they *have* a phone in that mausoleum! Fancy as it is, I had the impression that they would send out messages by carrier pigeon. So if you need me, old girl, send a pigeon—or if it seems wise, I'll call on you in person."

There was more, most of it nonsense, but all very welcome.

I reached my own particular beach and sat gazing back at the watching windows of the house. All was quiet, except for the hoarse cry of a gull flying out over the ocean. The fog was being threatened by a silver sun, which, while I watched, came out to make shadows on shade, and a slight wind stirred the pampas grasses and weeds nearby. I could have been alone in the world so far as sight and sound were concerned. I opened my book, *Far in the Night*, and began to explore the beginnings of a murder mystery.

The author was clever, spinning her tale with all the intricacies of a spider weaving his web, ever larger and larger, until he should lie in wait at its center for his prey.

I was being led, firmly and inexorably, toward the climax when I heard a sound above me, and rose from my half-reclining position to look.

A shaggy-looking man in brown flowing robes was plodding along, leaning on a staff. So incongruous was his appearance that he might have been a monk from the century of St. Francis. Except that he was not a monk, I thought. More of a mythical hermit. His feet were encased in rough sandals, his ankles bare. He did not seem aware of my presence, and I lay quietly watching him until he was out of sight of my sheltered cove. Then I rose and, keeping well down, ran up the dunes to see his destination. Where had he come from and how had he entered the Regent acres? I resolved to see where he was going, then explore back the way he had come to satisfy my own curiosity. I was still under the spell of the book and, although I shrugged the supposition away impatiently, I felt that he carried an aura of evil with him.

He approached Regent Manor as though he knew exactly where he was going, without haste but with a kind of inflexible determination. Now and then, he lifted his head to gaze at the windows, and I could see in his profile that his face was covered with coarse, curly hair. Were there mendicants in this part of the world? He might be a beggar from some nearby monastery soliciting fare for his needy dependents. Charles had said that there were many missions near here, and I had seen some of them on our trip, but I was curious, nevertheless.

He went to the back of the house where the storerooms and kitchens were. I had been down to the pantry to arrange my bouquets but was unfamilar with all the connected rooms. As he approached, a door swung wide and, unless my eyes deceived me from this distance, Vivian walked out to meet him. Whoever his welcoming companion, undoubtedly a female, they engaged in deep conversation for several minutes before he followed her into the house.

It was fairly easy to follow his footsteps in the sand, still damp from the early-morning fog. I walked slowly, laughing inwardly at myself for my sleuthing. His sandal marks seemed queer—very broad but short. I tried to fit my own feet into them, and was astounded at their breadth. It seemed that I had walked a long way, probably a mile or more, when I came to a mashed-down row of sagebrush beside a fence, on the other side of which cows grazed peacefully. This must be the end of the Regent acreage, I thought. Apparently, the visitor had climbed over the fence and landed rather clumsily in the brush. Because of the alfalfa, no tracks were discernible on the other side of the fence.

However, I was in an exploratory mood, and I followed the fence to the east, examining it from time to time for strength. It was about six feet high and reinforced with redwood over the wire—a cyclone fence, we used to call it back in Kansas. It was very sturdy and there was no gate anywhere along its length. At one point, I climbed up on a boulder to peek on the other side. My fingers found a sign, which I read upside down. It said in large letters, *No Trespassing*.

The monk had seemed sure of himself and of his admittance to Regent Manor. He had been welcomed by some member of the household. Even so, I thought I ought to call this to Jock's attention. After all, if everyone had made such a fuss about my own trespassing when I was expected, he might want to know of this other trespasser, too.

I was on my way back, traversing the high road where the monk had walked, when I happened to glance down at my portion of the beach and saw a slim young figure dancing in and out of the lacy water along the shore. *Annette!*

I couldn't mistake her lithe body, or the long hair that was copper-colored in the sun. She resembled a water nymph, running after the froth, then laughing as she ran away from its feeble encroachments toward her bare feet. She wore a white, shapeless shift, without sleeves, and her arms were evenly tanned.

I went down the promontory toward her quietly, not wishing to startle her. When I was fairly close, I called her name.

She paused for one startled second like a fawn in flight, then came running toward me, a timid and beautiful smile on her face.

"Hello, Annette."

"Hello," she said shyly.

"Where have you been all this time?" I asked, taking her hand and holding it in both of mine. "I've looked for you."

She disengaged her hand and pointed to the house. "Up there."

"I haven't seen you."

"I came to your door one night, but you were asleep. I mustn't disturb anybody."

"I see. I'm sorry to have missed you. I'll tell you what—it's nearly lunchtime. Why don't you come with me and we'll eat together on the terrace?"

At once, she hung back. "I can't," she said with a vigorous shake of her head.

"Then I'll go up to the house and get us a picnic

lunch, shall I? We'll eat it down here on our own special beach."

This time, she nodded, a sweet smile breaking over her lovely features. "I'll wait for you. Please come back."

I had no idea whether she was allowed to cavort at will on the beach, but, reassuring myself as to her safety, I ran up the dunes and took the high road to the kitchens. Never having been there, I knocked rather timidly.

The cook, Delphia, whom I had never seen, whisked open the door and glared at me for a moment before she exclaimed in a hearty voice, "Lord bless us, it's you, is it? I thought it might be somebody else, and I was about to loosen my tongue at the likes of him snooping around."

"I did see a man," I said, "coming this way." I watched her florid face carefully for any expression. "He looked like a—monk."

"Him!" she scoffed. "That's no holy monk, and that I can tell you by the sign of the cross." She interrupted herself to make that sign piously from forehead to breast, from shoulder to shoulder. "That's the devil's own, that one. A plague be on him!"

"He came inside," I ventured further.

"I'll take the broom to him—and to her, too—if ever I find the pair of them in my kitchen. What'll you be having, dearie—your lunch, maybe?"

"Yes. I thought I'd take it to the beach."

"Ah, then, wait there in the shade while I fix you a tasty bite."

Annette was straining her eyes toward the promontory when I returned. She ran to meet me, making those odd little mewing sounds when she saw the neat packet of food that Cook had prepared for us. We sat down side by side on a hillock and she leaned her sweet young body against me while we examined the cold fried chicken, cole slaw, and butter sandwiches. I gave her first choice, noticing again how ravenous she was and how she pulled the drumstick through her teeth, hardly pausing to swallow.

"You'll choke, darling," I said. "Eat it this way, see?"

I bit with exaggerated daintiness into a chicken thigh and chewed methodically while she watched. She did the same, her pretty white teeth showing, her eyes laughing into mine for approval.

"That's right." I praised her as one would a child. "Now a bite of bread—nicely now, darling."

She was so receptive to suggestion that I felt my heart melt toward her lovableness. We chewed together, laughing into each other's eyes as though it were all an enchanting new game. I poured milk and gave the glass to her, while I drank from the carton, both of us still smiling. And when the chicken and sandwiches were finished, I said, continuing to play the game, "And 'way down here in the bottom of the sack is a great big surprise!"

Annette clapped her hands together in glee and peeked inside. Then she took her frosted cake and began to dance all about in the sand, chanting pretty little sounds. Her eyes were not vacant now, nor afraid. She was a happy child, loving and beloved, nibbling daintily as she danced, her beautifully proportioned body swaying as gracefully as that of a ballerina. The cake was nearly consumed when suddenly she stopped in a pirouette, looking beyond me in wide-eyed fear. I rose to stare in the same direction, and I saw the brown-robed mendicant bearing down on us, or so I thought. Instinctively, without knowing why, I pushed Annette behind me, ready to face this source of her fear with violence if need be. I picked up a length of gnarled driftwood and lifted it threateningly, but the man passed several feet above without being aware of us. When he was out of sight, Annette clung to me, whimpering.

"Darling," she said on a small gasp. "Darling."

"Darling," I repeated after her, touched to the depths of my being. "Precious little darling, don't be afraid."

"Darling," she said again, and a smile blossomed through the tears.

"Who is he, Annette?"

She shook her head from side to side. "Bad man!"

I hesitated to question her further, but somehow I was thankful that I had been with her when the bearded man passed.

CHAPTER 5

Charles wrote to ask me if I might have Sunday off to have dinner with him in Carmel.

The weeks had gone by so quickly that I was not particularly anxious to disrupt the harmony. However, I felt that I owed Charles something for standing by me in a moment of very real need, so I took the letter to Mrs. Regent.

She had been dressed this morning in a lovely flowing housecoat, which covered her infirmities, and now she was sitting at her desk going over her mail. A warm sea-scented breeze flirted with the curtains, sucking them in close, then letting them billow softly into the room. Outside on the balcony, tubs of japonica, flouncy red petunias, and blue lobelia sent their own fragrance into the room.

"Oh, there you are!" Mrs. Regent said in her throaty voice. "And just in time, too. Oh, we do have the most fascinating bundle of letters this morning. Look here!" She displayed an envelope with a welter of foreign-looking stamps on the right-hand corner. "I've been saving these hoping that you and I might start a collection. Wouldn't that be interesting?"

"Very," I agreed with a smile. "I'll ask Jock to bring us an album the next time he is in the village." My own letter I tucked back into my skirt pocket; I could see that she wanted to get at the answers immediately. She began to dictate, reading each letter slowly.

"My dear Jacques, Yes, I am still in my mountain retreat, *mon ami*—" With each reply, she gave me a brief sketch of the recipient, of her association with him, and inserted detailed incidents and events, some of them humorous, some poignant. It was nearly noon before we had finished, and Mrs. Regent leaned back with a tired sigh.

"Would you ring for Vivian, please? I am ready for my lunch and my nap. This has been a particularly stimulating morning."

"I have had an invitation," I said, "to spend Sunday in Carmel."

"Oh?" Her fine brows lifted in inquiry and there was a faint smile on her lovely face. "Some young man, I daresay, who thinks we've kept you cooped up far too long?"

"He is a friend from home," I volunteered, "whom I ran into quite accidentally on my arrival in San Francisco. He offered me a drive down, and—"

"Oh yes," she said brightly, "the young man who helped you over the gates on the night of the storm. Mrs. Livingston dismissed him rather unceremoniously, I'm afraid." She pleated the lace frill at her wrist nervously before she said, "Why don't you ask him to dinner here on Sunday? I spoke of entertaining, remember? We may as well begin on this small scale."

"If it wouldn't be an imposition," I said with a smile.

Again, she hesitated, turning the matter over in her mind, apparently. Then she said, quite firmly, "Leave it to me, my dear Marly. Anything out of the ordinary seems to distress the household staff, but I'll attend to it, I assure you. Jock will take you in to Carmel to meet your friend— Oh, do go to the Mission! It is one of the finest, I believe—always reminded me of Spain. I used to go there regularly when I was in residence here. But that was so long ago, and now—*now* I have another kind of faith. My doctor has given it to me."

"Your doctor?" I repeated. "I have wanted to confer with him, Mrs. Regent, but he hasn't called, has he?"

"Do ring for Vivian," she said with faint irritation, "and we'll discuss medical matters another time. Right now, I must make arrangements for Sunday. We'll have music for— What is his name, my dear?"

"Charles Christian. But I don't want to tire you, Mrs. Regent. We can just as well have the day together and I can come back alone for our dinner together."

"Nonsense! If I don't soon break through this shell of invalidism, I'll never get well." She looked down at her useless fingers and flexed them with obvious pain. "I must get back to my piano, do you understand? And I will! With you here, encouraging me and giving me glimpses of your own youth and courage, I'll soon be running my scales."

This burst of optimism left me startled and speechless. Surely Mrs. Regent's physician had made it clear to her that she was the victim of rheumatoid arthritis, crippled, and not likely ever to improve. Certainly not to play the piano again. I turned my face away so that she would not read my disbelief in such a miracle. What kind of doctor had allowed this valiant and wonderful woman to think for an instant that she would be able to one day play her piano? She still had some use of her fingers, but it was an effort for her to use her knife and fork at the dinner table.

And I knew from experience that this condition would grow worse, not better. Certainly it would have been unprofessional for me, as a nurse, to deny the allegations of my patient's physician. At the first opportunity I was determined, however, to meet him and discuss this puzzling case frankly. Even if he thought it to be psychosomatic, I did not. In my opinion, Mrs. Regent was much too well adjusted and intelligent to force herself into disability, even though she had had some traumatic losses. No, I would close my mind to any idea of that kind.

Annette had acquired the habit of waiting for me on the beach for my afternoon walks, sometimes hiding in the pampas until I approached, then jumping out at me with childish giggles, often sliding down the sand from the promontory almost into my lap. I always pretended to be startled, then welcomed her with joyful surprise. This never failed to please her. Today, I wandered farther along the dunes, seeking her and listening. I had come almost to the cyclone fence that marked the property line when I saw her.

She was scratched and her legs skinned from scaling the high fence, and when she saw me, she ran forward, both arms outstretched, her face white with some unnamed terror.

"Annette!" I gathered her close. "Darling, what's the matter? Did you see a snake?"

She shook her head emphatically, clinging to me, her body trembling.

"Then what is it?" I persisted. "Tell Marly."

Somehow in our sketchy association Annette had confused my name with the endearment "darling." Now she jerked her head back to stare at me reproachfully. "Darling," she said with a frown, "not Marly."

"All right," I agreed indulgently, "tell 'Darling.'"

She took my hand and led me to the fence. There was a small knot missing in the redwood plank, and she gestured toward it and told me to peek through.

On the other side, at some distance, I saw a new and rather elegant house trailer of the kind used by many people for permanent homes. It still sat on wheels and the tracks were fresh through the alfalfa to show that it had been transported recently. But there was no car in sight.

"That's nothing to be afraid about," I said to her. "It's only a house on wheels."

"Bad man lives there," she insisted petulantly. She had once called the brown-robed mendicant a "bad man," I remembered. Did she mean that the ragged, bearded monk had come here to stay? I peeked through the hole again to make sure. A squat man in a blue shirt and trousers was pushing some large boulders under the wheels to keep the trailer stationary.

"That's not the bad man, dear," I said rather sharply. "That's a stranger—someone we've never seen before."

This time, Annette was most vehement. *Bad man, bad man!* she insisted, stamping her foot. "Bad man come here to get me, Darling! Make him go away!"

Her fright was not feigned, but real. I took her hand and drew her away from the fence where the man could not possibly overhear us. Then I sat Annette down and questioned her carefully.

"What happened? Did you go to visit, and make the man angry?"

She nodded vigorously. "I told him to go away— far away. He wouldn't listen, so I climbed over the fence and got a big stick to make him go."

I had picked up a stick of driftwood, I recalled, on the day the monk seemed to be coming toward us on the beach. I smiled to myself. Evidently my little friend had assumed that this was the way to treat all strangers.

"You shouldn't have done that, dear. That man is on the other side of the fence, not on our land. He is a *neighbor!*"

Neighbor, friend, stranger—I realized the limited scope of Annette's vocabulary. Who in the world was responsible for her and her education? Why didn't she know the meaning of the simplest words? She was bright, receptive, easy to teach— Where had she been all her life that she knew so little? I decided to try to find out.

"Annette," I said, mouthing my words carefully now that she was calmer, "where do you sleep—live?"

She looked at me as though I were insufferably stupid and waved an arm toward the Manor. "I sleep there. Why?"

"Where is your room? Upstairs, or down?"

Again the frown creased her brow. "Up," she said in growing bewilderment.

"Do you know who Mrs. Livingston is?"

"Yes," she said, still bewildered. Then she hopped to her feet and did a brilliant imitation of the housekeeper's waddle. I laughed, and she continued, glad to have pleased me.

"All right," I said. "That's enough of that foolishness. Now, tell me, do you know Vivian and Jock?"

She nodded. "Yes, yes," she said impatiently. "And Rose and Kate and Cook." Her eyes took on a faraway look as she added, "And Michael."

"Tell me about Michael," I prompted with carefully controlled eagerness.

She began to trail her fingers along a juniper bush, tearing at the thorny fronds in something like annoyance. "Michael went away."

"Michael went away? When?"

Annette shrugged. I had lost her limited attention and now she was pawing at my pockets for the "surprise" I usually brought to her from my luncheon tray. She found the macaroon and several figs, and devoted herself to consuming them daintily, smiling all the time to herself.

"You're a little rogue," I told her fondly. "I think you construct these fairy tales of yours out of whole cloth. But you're smart enough, aren't you, to make a good tale out of it?"

I had lost her interest completely now, and she ran along the beach ahead of me, her fright forgotten in her joy. Her shapeless little shift looked cleaner today, I noticed, and her hair seemed smoother than usual. Did she—could she—know how extraordinarily lovely she was? Perfectly uninhibited, she ran into the water where it laced the shore, and came back to me like a frolicking puppy to seize my hand and whisper, "Darling!" Oh, how adorable she was! How innocent and tender! Who was she, and to whom did she belong?

For the first time in my life, I wanted this child, wanted to protect her, to open new vistas of learning to her, to love her and care for her. She was delightful, a minx with mixtures of humor and fears that governed her queer little antics. And she trusted me and loved me— Why did no one in the big house on the cliff ever mention her name?

"Annette, does Mrs. Livingston feed you and—and keep your clothes?" I asked when she had calmed down and was walking sedately beside me. "Who cares for you?"

Her eyes slanted into a teasing expression and she shook her head. "I won't tell! I won't tell!" she chanted, charging up the dunes. "Chase me!"

It was no use. I simply could not get through to her in this elfin mood. We played for a while until she lost interest, then I left her, pondering the mystery.

Of course I could not distress Mrs. Regent with a tale of a strange waif who gamboled on her beaches each day and slept under her roof, for I was convinced that she knew nothing of all this. Her windows did not look down on the sea, nor had she ever mentioned any knowledge of Annette. Some instinct told me not to ask the Livingstons, either. But what about Delphia, the cook? She had been quite volatile on the one occasion I had seen her. What was it she had said about the friar? That he was no man of God!

Rose and Kate were little nonentities who, when they spoke at all, giggled nervously. I couldn't imagine approaching either of them with my questions and receiving any satisfaction as to Annette's history. Who was she? Where did she come from, and why was she here? She couldn't possibly belong to any of the servants; she was too lovely and graceful, too fair.

So it was with my questions unanswered that I went on Sunday to meet Charles at the Pine Inn in Carmel. He looked so blessedly normal coming toward me across the lobby, so handsome and citified in his cashmere jacket and matching slacks, that I could only return his affectionate greeting with my own.

"Have you had breakfast?" he asked immediately. "You have? Then let's get going. I have so much to show you, so much to hear and say. Ah, Marly, you look like a flower!"

"First, the Mission," I said. "I promised Mrs. Regent. Then you shall have your own way. Oh, and you are invited to dinner tonight at the Manor!"

"Really! Now *this* will be something to tell my grandchildren! Are the ghosts still rattling their chains, and how's the old battle-ax who gave me the bawling-out?"

We were on the way to the car at the curb, his arm on mine urging me along, when I saw Jock across the street loading supplies into the pickup. He stopped, his wily old eyes squinted against the early-morning sun, and regarding us with something like hate. *Why, what's the matter with Jock?* I thought. He had been quietly amiable this morning on our trip to town. Now he was like a stranger, glaring balefully. I felt a chill as I settled into Charles's bullet-car.

The day was a montage of sea and sun, of gentle green hills and curving countryside. We had lunch in a valley bowl overshadowed by a range of blue-green mountains, and talked ourselves hoarse. Charles had been seeing BJ, he told me, and thought she was quite a Spartan type of girl.

"Lots of moxie," he said. "She comes on strong, though, and I'll admit she leaves me cut and bleeding with that rapier wit. You're a relief, darling, after coping with BJ."

I laughed in amusement. I could have told him that my erstwhile schoolmate was a man-eater, but that would have spoiled it for him. And just when he thought he had discovered someone unique, too. "You'll manage," I told him. "How's business coming?"

"Hiring and firing," he said indifferently. "What else is there? I only hang around at this point because you're somewhere near. Why don't you let me take you out of all this, Marly? It must be deadly dull for you."

"Dull?" I cried. "You've got to be kidding! Some new mystery unfolds daily." I told him about the "doctor" I never saw and his peculiar influence on Mrs. Regent. It was not until I described my darling Annette, though, that I aroused his attention in my new life.

"Cracked, you say? Must be an illegitimate child —perhaps of the maid's, Vivian."

"It isn't funny, Charles," I protested. "She's very bright, actually, but totally uneducated. And she's beautiful! No, you're wrong, Sherlock, about Vivian's being her mother. Vivian's dark and moody and—yes, ugly. This girl—I can't imagine her having ordinary parents. She seems spawned from the sea—a sprite, and so lovable, too."

"Well," he said practically, "suppose we get at the bottom of it tonight. I'll simply ask the old lady about her."

"No, please don't do that!" I remonstrated, thinking of Jock's peculiar behavior. "There is an odd climate of mistrust prevalent, and I—I wouldn't want them to think I'm snooping. There's the 'doctor' whom I've never seen, although I'm engaged as Mrs. Regent's nurse. Then, too, there is Michael Davidson, whom I've never seen."

"And the child, Annette, whom you're not supposed to know is in existence. I say, Marly, you *have* bitten off quite a chunk, you know. Why do you stay on?"

"I'm fascinated, I guess. Everything is so delightfully normal most of the time. Then I run into odd little matters—like the man in the trailer who frightened Annette so badly." I told him about the incident, but Charles was more interested in Annette's identity than any of my other "mysterics."

"That youngster," he kept saying, "has a story to tell if only one could get it out of her."

"I don't think so," I disagreed. "Whatever the story might be, Annette is not conscious of it. She's too affectionate and fun-loving. You should see how she entertains herself, Charles, with the simplest of nature's joys. You'd adore her! I do, except that I find myself wanting to acquaint her with—things."

"The complexities of life?" he jeered. "Forget it, my sweet! As long as she is happy, don't disturb the equilibrium."

"But she's so lovely! She ought to be going to parties, like other girls her age.

"That would be like throwing her to the wolves, wouldn't it?"

"I suppose so. But I'd like to be the one to take her to her first movie. Or something," I ended lamely.

"The Lord forbid!" Charles said fervently.

We spent the greater part of the afternoon on a tidy little nine-hole golf course, Charles insisting that he needed the exercise to combat the dullness of office routine and the deadly fog of the city. He very generously gave me nine strokes because I had no known handicap, and I beat him unmercifully, much to his chagrin.

"That'll teach you to underestimate a mere woman," I teased him. "Next time, we'll play for stakes."

We were still laughing about it when Charles drew up to the gates, which had been left open for us. He raised his eyebrows at this and took the climb slowly to the portico. "So they've reinforced the fence to keep me out," he said grimly, "if I should ever want to storm the castle again."

"If you do," I said, "there is an easier way at the north end of the property. Apparently, the monk I told you about mounts a large flat stone on the other side and drops down onto the pampas. I saw the imprint of his trespass."

"Very good. I'll tuck that gem of information away for future use."

Mrs. Regent was not down yet, so I took Charles to the library. Evening fog was crowding against the French windows like a thick white blanket. A fire burned merrily on the hearth, and after showing him the bar and telling him to mix himself a drink, I went upstairs to freshen up for dinner.

Someone had been in my rooms!

Bric-a-brac had been disarranged on the tables and drawers were left open, their contents scattered. In the bedroom, the havoc was even worse. My lingerie had been carefully shaken out in a search and then thrown on the bed and floor. Even the bathroom had been invaded. Annette? At first, I was inclined to blame her, for I knew her mercurial moods. If she had come to see me and found me gone, she might have had one of her flashing little temper tantrums. For this reason, I tidied up the mess and resolved to say nothing.

But when I went downstairs again, I found someone else, a man, before the fire with Mrs. Regent and Charles. He was leaning against the mantel with negligent grace, his back toward the door. I stopped short as I heard Mrs. Regent's soft laugh.

Immediately, the stranger turned to me and our eyes met in a long, scrutinizing look before Mrs. Regent said gaily, "Marly, this is Michael Davidson. Marly Carewe, Michael. Well, now isn't this an unexpected surprise?" she went on when we nodded briefly. "Only the other day I was telling Marly that we must entertain again, and"—she lifted her shoulders —"the matter seems to have been taken out of our hands by the gods. Two such attractive young men at once! Marly dear, you do look radiant! A day in the open has done wonders for you. Mr. Christian, you must get her away more often."

Charles plunged into the suggestion without ado. "I thought I might ask Marly to the city during the opera season," he said appreciatively, "if you can spare her. Her friend BJ is an artist of sorts and can put her up."

While this exchange was going on, Mrs. Regent reminiscing about the brilliance of the opera season, I was free to observe Michael Davidson. He was tremendously attractive, I thought. His hair was sandy, almost red, and the tawny eyes under heavy brows regarded me curiously. Their expression was wary, although his mouth smiled, and I felt as though I were under some kind of suspicion.

"I'm told that you know Dr. Burley," I said tentatively, embarrassed by his scrutiny. "I believe that he and your father were classmates at med school."

"I believe my father trusted Dr. Burley implicitly," he said significantly. "But no, I have never met the doctor. We've corresponded sporadically through the years since my father's death."

I felt somewhat flattened, not so much by his denial of knowing Dr. Burley as by his rather cold statement of his father's trust in him. It was as though, seeing me, his own trust in his father's friend was somewhat shaken.

Fortunately, Mrs. Livingston chose this moment to appear and announce dinner. Usually this was done by a gong, but I could see that Mrs. Livingston was in rare spirits tonight. She beamed at Michael, and as I went to Mrs. Regent's side to assist her from her chair, I heard him say to her, "You've done yourself proud tonight, Livvie."

"I didn't mind at all, Michael, with *you* here."

They seemed to be on familiar, even affectionate, terms. Immediately, Michael came to Mrs. Regent, almost pushing me aside, to help her to her feet. I noticed that he let her lean on his arm, his hand on hers, as they began the laborious walk down the long entry hall to the dining room.

Mrs. Livingston had, indeed, done herself proud. The immense crystal chandelier sent its rays down on stiff, spotless damask, where flowers, silver, and wine-glasses sparkled in festive array. Rose was faultlessly uniformed in black with a small white apron tied at her slim waist. She repressed a giggle as Michael spoke to her and pulled the thronelike chair out for Mrs. Regent. Jock, too, had been pressed into duty. He was scrubbed and pinkly polished, and only slight-ly incongruous in his dull-green livery as he presided over the wine.

Mrs. Regent lifted her glass. "To the beginning of a new life modeled after the old."

Michael said something to her under his breath, and she tapped him lightly on the wrist. "This boy," she said, "takes liberties. But I like it. His mother and I were schoolmates long ago at Miss—what ever was that name now, Michael? Oh yes, Miss Hedges. How could I have forgotten? Michael was several years younger than my dear Sylvia, and I'm afraid she teased him terribly."

"I loved Sylvia, Aunt Marian," Michael interposed. "I missed her like anything when you whisked her away."

Charles was listening to this exchange, his ears prac-tically pointing like a setter's to glean a clue to the mysteries. His foot brushed mine under the table as though telling me to let them *talk* without interrup-tion.

"Ah, yes, how the years did fly!"

"And your daughter?" Charles broke in.

"She died fourteen years ago," Michael said tersely. "My father attended her in her last illness—in New York."

Mrs. Regent dabbed at her eyes, and the sad sub-ject was dropped when Michael turned to me and asked, "Is this your first visit to the West, Miss Ca-rewe?"

"Oh dear, let's not be formal, Michael," Mrs. Regent protested, regaining her composure. "Now that you're back, you'll be with us often, I hope. I want you and Marly to be great friends." Charles's foot touched mine again with slightly more pressure while Mrs. Regent continued: "Michael is like a son to me, and has been ever since the deaths of his own parents and my daughter. I guess we rather gravitated together in our loss, didn't we, Michael? Unfortunately for me, he is a scientist and lecturer, which takes him to all sorts of places." She turned to him with a fond smile. "Where was it this time, dear boy?"

Mrs. Livingston brought in the main course under a silver salver and placed it before Mrs. Regent for approval. Michael Davidson answered only after the brief inspection. "Majorca, Aunt Marian. Before that, I was in Mexico."

The dinner conversation turned to Mexico, its people and customs. Charles told an amusing story of a trip to Oaxaca, and Michael responded with one of his own. I remained silent, wanting, like Charles, to absorb as much information about this newcomer as possible. Evidently he was a favorite with all the members of the household, and like a son to Mrs. Regent. Annette had spoken of him with familiarity, too. But there was something about him, slightly suspicious and disapproving, and more than once I caught his glance across the table as though he were assessing me, my motives and judging my sincerity. He had reported Mrs. Regent to be in financial distress in his letter to Dr. Burley, but surely the reverse was true. I had seen no signs of penury since I had been under this magnificent roof, and I wondered at his deception.

After an hour of music and more conversation in the library, Vivian was summoned to help Mrs. Regent upstairs. I noticed how awkward her aid was in comparison to Michael's earlier gentleness. I saw him look at me as though I were remiss in not attending to the invalid myself, and I answered the question in his eyes before he could phrase it.

"Mrs. Regent prefers Vivian to assist her," I said. "Sometimes I go in for a chat after she is in bed, though, while she has her hot milk."

"Odd," he said in some perplexity. "I wonder why."

"Vivian seems to be oversensitive where Mrs. Regent is concerned. We discussed the matter briefly, and Mrs. Regent prefers it this way."

"I see," he said in that same puzzled tone. "Vivian was always a morose type, even as a child. I should have thought that Aunt Marian would prefer having you about."

"Apparently, Mrs. Regent is most considerate of everyone's feelings," Charles said. "She is a charming lady."

"And a great one, yes." Michael addressed me: "What do you think of her condition?"

"Professional ethics forbid me to say much," I hedged, "since I have not seen her doctor. I understand that he has called to see her, but I was not aware of this at the time."

He made an exclamation that sounded like an oath. "Don't tell me that quack is still coming around?"

I looked at Charles in complete mystification, but he, too, was waiting for my reply. "I have no knowledge of his credentials," I said coldly, "nor have I heard his name."

For one so relaxed, so almost lazy in his mannerisms, Michael Davidson rose to full fury. "Miss Carewe, you are here to *care* for her! You're a *nurse*, aren't you?"

CHAPTER 6

Some time later, I was alone with Charles when I walked him to the car. Still smarting under Michael's implication that I had neglected my patient, I intended, on Charles's departure, to go back to the library and have an understanding with him on the matter. I had been hired as a nurse, to be sure, and was, myself, a bit piqued at having minor duties thrust upon me. But somehow it had not been apparent how much laxity had prevailed in my present duty until Michael Davidson's irate question.

"He's the father," Charles hissed when we were well away from the imposing portals.

Engrossed in my own problems, I did not, at first, realize what he was talking about.

"He's the father of the girl," Charles repeated, and then it dawned on me that he meant Annette.

"Don't be silly, Charles. Annette is fourteen, or so, and Michael Davidson can't be much more than thirty."

"Hm-m," Charles said thoughtfully. Then he brightened. "He's much too old for you, Marly. Steer clear of him, won't you? He behaved abominably just now. Who does he think he is? All that 'dear-boy' stuff doesn't give him the right to abuse you. If Mrs. Regent is satisfied, that's an end to it, wouldn't you say?"

"I suppose I should have stayed nearer the house,"

I said speculatively, "in case she needed me. But actually, my duties are more those of a paid companion, while she seems to prefer to have Vivian bathe and dress her. Another peculiar thing, Charles—she takes no medication."

"Hm-m," Charles said again. "I wonder why? She must have pain with those swollen joints. I noticed that her hands gave her some discomfort tonight at dinner. But she manages well."

"Yes. Well, now that you've seen us all assembled, what do you think?"

Charles leaned on the car in contemplation. "I'd have said not too much to be concerned about, at least until that chap Davidson showed up. He puzzles me, for all his hearty good cheer. Do you feel it?"

"I think," I said, "that he is some kind of administrator. At least, he manages Mrs. Regent's affairs—or implied that he did in his letter to Dr. Burley. One thing titillates me, though. He said that she was in financial straits and at the same time named a quite generous salary. Do you suppose he is subsidizing her for some reason?"

"Not on a scientist-lecturer's income," Charles said firmly. "His devotion to her seems real enough, but I thought he rather slid over the matter of Sylvia's death. What did she die *of?* I say, wasn't it terribly sudden for anyone that young, and in apparent good health—good enough, anyway, for her to make a long journey to be with her mother? Then, to pop off in New York so suddenly on her way here."

"Oh that! It could have been anything—heart, for instance. Even if she'd had any knowledge of cardiac weakness, she wouldn't have let her mother know, would she?"

"Did she have any children? Could Annette be *hers?*" Charles snapped his fingers in discovery.

"That's it! Annette's the offspring of the dead daughter and her husband!"

"I—don't—know," I said slowly. "I've never seen any pictures of Mrs. Regent's daughter in her rooms. However, Annette does have the same general coloring as Mrs. Regent. But then," I laughed, "you and I look enough alike to be relatives. In fact, the first time I saw you I was struck by your likeness to my brother Matt."

"The way I feel about you isn't at all fraternal," he said, pulling me toward him.

"No, Charles, please, not here!" I extricated myself, conscious of the watching windows. "Getting back to the daughter, doesn't it strike you as odd that Mrs. Regent doesn't have pictures of Sylvia since they were so devoted? And if you *should* be right, and Annette *is* Mrs. Regent's granddaughter, wouldn't you imagine that she would dote on the girl?"

"Doesn't seem to know she's around, eh?"

"She has never mentioned her to me, although she has commented on and discussed the other members of the household. No, I'm convinced that Mrs. Regent doesn't know that Annette exists."

"What about Davidson? You said that the girl mentioned him, didn't you?"

"Yes, and with a queer mixture of anxiety and familiarity. She wanted to know if he was her friend. Oh well, it's all too mixed up to solve in one evening. You go along now, Charles. It has been a lovely day, but I don't think we ought to do it again until I've cleared up some of my doubts here. In fact, when Mr. Davidson gets finished with me this evening, I may be looking for another job."

"You stick with Mrs. Regent," Charles said solemnly. "I have a feeling she's going to need you. And call me if anything unusual comes up, will you, darling? And take care of yourself, hear? I'll be in touch."

I watched his car down the lane and out of sight, then turned back to the house. On my way, I noticed that Jock had been waiting in the shadows for Charles's departure so that he could lock the gates after him. Again, I remembered the malice in his face as he had glared at us this morning in the village. Had he overheard our talk just now?

Michael was still in the library, having a brandy which he swished around in the snifter. The fire was low and the hour late, but I wanted to have this out with him once and for all.

"Mr. Davidson, I have not intentionally neglected my duties to my patient," I began rather stiffly.

He reached out one foot and used it to pull another chair closer to his before the fire. "Pour yourself a brandy," he said without rising, "and sit down."

I sat down on the edge of the chair, but I did not pour a brandy. "Mrs. Regent herself delegated my duties on my first morning here."

His smile was amused. "Oh! And what are those duties, may I ask?"

I flushed under his amused scrutiny, realizing that I was trapped by trivialities. If I said flower arranging and letter-writing, he would think me a fool, and incompetent as well. There was no help for it, however.

"She likes my company for breakfast," I said. "After that, while Vivian is taking care of her and dressing her hair for the day, I get the mail from Jock and wait. When Vivian has finished and the rooms have been straightened, we go through the mail and Mrs. Regent dictates her replies to the letters."

"I see." He pretended to be deeply absorbed in the brandy glass, moving it between the palms of his hands to warm it. "These letters—do you see them?"

I bridled. "Certainly not! She reads me portions at times, that's all."

"And are a great many of them from France?"

"What difference does it make?" I flared. "If you wish to know about Mrs. Regent's correspondence, you may ask her yourself. Her personal mail remains in confidence as far as I am concerned."

"Good girl!" he said unexpectedly. "You're all right!" He got to his feet with that catlike grace and took my hand to lift me to mine. "I'll be here several days, and it's late now for talk. But you and I will go into the matter of Aunt Marian's personal welfare tomorrow or another day." He hesitated, again giving me that look of appraisal. "She is frequently a victim of her own impulsiveness. I'm concerned for her— *safety*."

The word shot through me like a bolt of lightning, and I looked to him for something further, but he was bent over the fire, stoking the ashes with a poker and shovel. There was nothing to do but say good night, which I did without further ceremony.

Mrs. Regent insisted on coming downstairs for breakfast the next morning. From my room, I could hear Vivian's scolding between Mrs. Regent's remarks, which were delivered in her usual calm and soothing tones. I stayed, waiting, so that I could help Vivian assist her down the long stairway. While I was lingering in the wide, sun-flooded hall, Michael Davidson came from his room at the other end.

"How now!" he greeted me. He looked unusually fit in white tennis shoes and ducks, a brown sweater pulled over the white shirt underneath. "Have I missed breakfast? I'm hungry as a horse."

"Good morning, Mr. Davidson. No, I'm waiting to

take Mrs. Regent down. She wants to have breakfast with us."

"Good enough," he agreed, rubbing his hands together in good humor. "Go on ahead, will you, and alert Livvie."

"Mrs. Livingston doesn't take orders from me," I reminded him.

"Then, tell her *I* said so," he said carelessly over his shoulder, making straight for Mrs. Regent's suite. "Tell her I said to shake it up."

I went downstairs knowing full well that I would do no such thing. There was no necessity. The table was set in the sunny breakfast room looking down over the precipice to the sea. On the buffet, tempting covered salvers were already arranged, and Rose was regulating the coffee urn. She greeted me pleasantly enough, but her eyes went beyond me to the entry hall as though she were looking for someone far more important than I. Michael? Of course! The "dear boy," as Charles had called him sarcastically, the scion of the family, was home. And while the house was usually in order and the service excellent, I saw that this morning everything was geared to the high standards of Mr. Michael Davidson's pleasure.

Why did they adore him so collectively? *I* hadn't found him all that lovable last night. Oh well, I conceded reluctantly, it might be that we had just got off on the wrong foot. Today I had hopes that we could gain each other's trust and confidence, and that I could unravel some of the mysteries of Regent Manor. For instance, the matters of Mrs. Regent's safety. Had he been referring to her health merely, or to another kind of danger? Who would want to hurt a dear lady who was so unfailingly kind?

And Annette—would he tell me who she was without my asking? One thing I had determined not to do: that was not to ask him for any information whatever. I would not have him think that I pried into affairs that were none of my business.

Mrs. Livingston appeared from nowhere when the mistress of the house entered the lovely windowed room. The housekeeper seemed to be charged with some kind of electricity, giving orders to Rose, pulling Mrs. Regent's chair out for her, beaming at Michael. Vivian exchanged a few whispered words with her mother, nodded, and shuffled from the room. It seemed odd that the contrast between them was so strong—the mother so starched and neat, while Vivian was so disreputable. I wondered that Michael did not notice it and, since he had so much influence with them all, make a few suggestions about her appearance.

Mrs. Regent was even more spirited than usual, too. She put a spoon into her melon and remarked that someone had gone early to the village to provide such a delectable meal. Her blue eyes were bluer than ever, and as they rested on the sliver of beach visible below the cliffs, I saw her straighten and peer more closely.

"Who on earth? Who is that girl on the beach, Michael?" There was curiosity, shock, and something like fear in her voice. "Has Jock let someone in here?"

"No, madam," Mrs. Livingston said quickly. "Certainly not!" She exchanged a meaningful look with Michael and went quickly to adjust the curtains, shutting out the sun. Had it been Annette? I wondered.

The meal continued, Michael relating news from their mutual acquaintances for Mrs. Regent and trying to distract her, it seemed, but I saw her eyes going back again and again to the slice of beach where I knew Annette loved to frolic. Michael simply went on chatting as he devoured his steak-and-kidney pie with relish.

"You'll spoil me," he said finally when he had finished and was leaning back in his chair. He lit a cigarette and asked, "What's on the agenda for this morning, Aunt Marian? I have some papers to go over with you if you feel up to it."

"Papers—papers!" Mrs. Regent said rather testily. "What is it now, Michael? Selling off more of my precious land?" She turned to me. "Kind and sweet as this dear boy is, he's a born pessimist. He persists in calling me extravagant! Imagine?" She gave a lilting little laugh. "You should have been with me, Michael, when I *really* spent money! Oh dear, the gowns, the jewels—suites at the finest hotels in Europe, town houses and country places—Sylvia's nannies and governesses, her riding master and ponies. Poor Jerome could never become accustomed to such affluence, bless him! And you, Michael, are an arch-conservative."

Michael continued to smile at her, saying nothing.

"But my heart was always here at Regent Manor," she went on to me. "We renamed it after my marriage to Jerome. He loved it here—the quiet and privacy for miles and miles. We had bridle trails then, you know, and horses, and while I practiced, he and our little girl would ride for hours."

"Sylvia taught me to ride," Michael said in a faraway voice. "When I was five, she boosted me up on a Shetland pony and gave him a swat on the rump and let us both go lickety-split down the beach. I can still hear the wind whistling in my ears while I held on like grim death."

"That was naughty of her," Mrs. Regent said, unperturbed. "She was a very headstrong girl in some ways, and completely helpless in others. I used to wonder after her marriage what kind of mother she would make with her mercurial moods. But, alas, that never came about, did it, Michael?"

A change came over Michael's face and the hand that crushed out his cigarette was unsteady. What was the matter with him? I thought, casting him a sharp look. Had he become suddenly ill? His mouth opened once or twice, but no sound came. I was about to rise from my chair and offer him a glass of water, when Mrs. Livingston bustled in and asked brightly, "Is everything all right? Is there anything more you'd like, madam?"

The mood had passed, whatever it was, and Michael rose to assist Mrs. Regent. They went to the library, where I could hear their voices rise and fall in normal tones, and were closeted there for hours.

I went down to the beach to look for Annette. It was she who was the key to all this deceit, I was convinced. If I could get her to talk, to recall any of her earlier memories, perhaps I could piece this puzzle together.

But Annette was nowhere about all that day.

CHAPTER 7

Had I had the opportunity, I would have asked Michael Davidson about Annette in the following days. The conference in the library had moved to Mrs. Regent's sitting room and there were no more "family breakfasts." In fact, I thought Mrs. Regent seemed wan and distracted during her evening appearances for cocktails and dinner, but I had found that any references to her health always annoyed her, so I kept my peace and watched.

Michael, when he was not in conference with her, or going over ledgers and papers in the library, drove off somewhere in his small foreign car, often not returning until long after dinner. Mrs. Regent seemed particularly nervous during these late absences. Once she asked me, apropos of nothing, "What do you think of Michael?"

"He is very attractive," I replied quite honestly. "And he seems to be most considerate."

"Lack of consideration has never been one of Michael's shortcomings," she agreed, "if, indeed, he has any. I'm glad you think him attractive. Personally, I don't know what I'd have done without him all these years, crippled and alone. He has devoted himself to me as though I were his own mother, and to tell the truth, my dear, he *is* my son. If not actually, at least by osmosis. But, like any mother, I worry about him."

She looked at me obliquely. "I hope you won't think me a meddling old fool, Marly, but I'm keenly concerned for his future. He is at an age when he should have been married for some years now. Yet I've never known Michael to show any interest whatever in any girl."

"He is very busy," I said in some embarrassment.

Her keen eyes never wavered from my face. "Not too busy to need love in his life," she said significantly. She seemed in a confidential frame of mind, so I lapsed into an attentive silence. "You are a clever girl and you may have wondered why I have a nurse when Vivian tends to all my needs. Michael says I'm impulsive, and so I am, but I've given the matter a great deal of thought, and, in a manner of speaking, I decided to let the mountain come to Mahomet. Since I was unable to entertain and arrange Michael's propinquity with nice and eligible girls, I asked him to find a nurse for me." She was breathing rather rapidly in her desire to explain to me. "That first morning I saw that you were all that I desired for him. Your graciousness, the way you handled my eccentricities, even the way your lovely hands lay so quietly, and—please don't misunderstand me, my dear—the fact that you did not have much money and are obliged to work for a living. I shouldn't want Michael to fall into the snare of a fortune-hunter, you know."

"Mrs. Regent—" I interrupted, my face scarlet.

"Now, now, my dear, please bear with me. I'm still in full possession of all my faculties. Michael will be a rich man when I am gone. He is my sole heir, except for bequests to my faithful friends, the Livingstons, and the other servants. I would like to know that he has made the right marriage and his happiness insured before I die."

"Mrs. Regent," I said, determined to put a stop to her fancies, "I scarcely know Mr. Davidson, nor he me. I'm sorry, but there could never be anything—"

She reached to take my hand. "Please don't say that, Marly. There is a Destiny of which we have only vague glimpses until that cataclysmic moment when, all at once, love steps in." She let my hand fall. "You'll think me an incurable romanticist, as perhaps I am. But everything in my own life bears out my theory. I could have married titles, remember? I was the darling of Europe at a time when many were feted and sought after. And then," a smile came over her face, reminding me of Annette's, "Jerome Regent walked into my life, rumpled, poor, and utterly without the social graces." She leaned forward in her eagerness. "He was so *real*, so sincere and gentle, and I knew he was the only man in the world for me!"

The antique clock on the mantel ticked on, the fire whispered, and I felt my own heart constrict. One never listens to the tender memories of a love that is gone, I think, without some sensation of pathos.

"Jerome and our daughter became the very center of my existence. I dreamed of the day when we could come back here for good and be together. The rest of the story you know. Just one more concert—and one more." She looked down at her hands. "I'll always be thankful that Jerome was gone before this happened —that he never saw me like this."

"And your daughter, Mrs. Regent?" I asked, delving into this mythical past that so intrigued me.

"Sylvia's was a similar love story. She married a soldier in the army of Her Majesty just before I was afflicted. Due to his long absences in his military career, she was able to be with me during the worst of my illness. And then he, too, died, the victim of a rare tropical disease. Poor Sylvia was distraught, I'm sure—and I couldn't be with her. She was detained for some months in England settling the estate."

"There were no children?"

"No, unfortunately, there were not. I came here with the Livingstons to open this house and get it ready to be a haven for my poor girl. I never saw her again, as you know."

She was in a reminiscent mood, and although I did not wish to distress her unnecessarily, I did want to hear the particulars of Sylvia's sudden death. I wanted, too, to keep her off the subject of Michael Davidson and myself. "Was there a coroner's verdict?"

The question startled her. Those questing eyes pierced into mine indignantly. "Certainly not! Why should there be? Sylvia became ill on the ship. She had chosen this way of travel at the suggestion of her physician, who felt that a sea trip would be beneficial."

"She had a physician, and yet she was not ill when she left England?" I pressed.

"Heartsick, yes, but not ill physically. Because of my own precarious health at that time, I was not notified of her illness, but Michael's father, Dr. Davidson, was. He met the ship and arranged for hospitalization. He sent for young Michael, and they were both with her at the end several days later. Dr. Davidson himself died a few years later of a massive coronary occlusion, and Michael and I were both left bereft."

"I suppose you had the particulars of your daughter's death?" I asked as casually as possible.

"Some people die of a broken heart," she said sadly. "Sylvia was like that—intense, passionately devoted to Clive. Yes, I'm sure that grief took her life."

"And Dr. Davidson's theory? Did he agree with your diagnosis of the cause of death?"

"I never saw him after that," she said sadly. "He and young Michael made all the arrangements for Sylvia's funeral—cremation, you know—and a few years later, Michael was called back to New York from college by the death of his father. And now, let us speak of other things, please. Is Mr. Christian the cause of your disinterest in Michael?"

This persistent woman was back on the subject again, and I knew that I was in for a bad time. I wondered if she had spoken in this vein to Michael. The thought made my face hot. He might even think that I had put her up to it.

"Charles is a friend," I said. "That, and nothing more."

"He is a very personable young man, I'm sure, and excessively devoted, I thought. Both Michael and I had the impression, however, that he was much more fond of you than you are of *him*." There was a teasing light in her eyes and a chiding smile on her lips. "Forgive me for prying, but am I right?"

"In these days, Mrs. Regent, there is a great deal of playing at love. You wouldn't understand that, and neither do I. Charles does. At the moment, he is fascinated by a girl I went to school with, Betty Jean Barnett—everyone calls her BJ."

"And I can see that it means nothing to you," Mrs. Regent said triumphantly. "You would not speak of it so indifferently if you were jealous."

The clock struck the half-hour after seven, and I drew a breath of relief that this disquieting interrogation must come to an end. But at that moment another voice was heard and Michael was in the room.

"I drove fast and furiously," he said, "to spend this last evening with you two." He nodded toward the cocktail tray. "Have I time for a quick one?"

"Of course, Michael," Mrs. Regent said warmly.

"We had almost given you up. And what's this about your 'last evening'?"

He tapped the breast pocket of his coat. "I'm scheduled for a lecture tour back East. The letter was waiting for me in my office today. Boston, Philadelphia, Washington, New York— A great chance, Aunt Marian, and one I've been craving for a long time. It seems that the scheduled lecturer—a brilliant archeologist whom I know slightly—has other commitments. So I am elected stand-in—a poor replacement, I might add."

"So you will be away—how long?" Mrs. Regent asked in apparent perturbation.

"Some weeks," he said negligently. "But I have your accounts in order, and Miss Carewe will be here to keep an eye on you."

I smiled back at him and nodded with perfect poise. *I'm glad you're going,* I thought. *There is something extraordinarily peculiar about Sylvia's death—and I'm sure you know it!*

Michael Davidson had no sooner gone, though, until I wished him back!

For one thing, Annette had disappeared completely!

Somehow I had not been too much concerned at not finding her on the beach while he was still at Regent Manor. I knew that she was shy and that she disliked any type of invasion. She lived in her own little world of simplicity and childishness, and I was not unduly concerned at her hiding herself away while there was a guest in the house.

But on the third day after Michael's departure, I became alarmed. Many times she hid from me, but always she came out at my call. Now there was no answer to my persistent calling of her name, no sweet stumbling into my arms at the promise of cakes or treats. If her constant hunger wouldn't bring her from a hiding place, I knew that she was gone.

But where?

I haunted the beach, walking miles up and down the property. I dreamed of her at night. She would be bruised and broken from a fall, or her body floating grotesquely at the edge of the lacy waves she loved. Anything could have happened to her, and I longed with all my heart to notify the village authorities and have them comb the wild and rugged area. Worse, there was no one to whom I could confide my anxieties. So far as I knew, only Mrs. Livingston knew of the girl's existence. So I approached her quite accidentally one morning.

"The night I came here," I said haltingly, "there was a girl on the stair."

Her button-brown eyes looked into mine with the innocence of a newborn babe. "One of the maids?"

"No. You called her 'Annette,' and you rather scolded her."

"More like Vivian, perhaps, peeking down to get a firsthand look at you. Vivian's oddly jealous, you know, of anything concerning her care of the mistress. Likely she was peeking to see what you looked like."

I felt that it was wise not to question her further, so I laughed. "I guess it was Vivian, at that," I said. "It was dark up there and I couldn't see too well."

"Yes, it must have been Vivian. She's a queer one, that girl, and jealous." I thought I detected a note of warning in her words.

I had another and more important quest—Delphia. At least the cook wasn't furtive. She had spoken her mind with Irish temper on the occasion of the mendicant's visit. Now if I could think of a good excuse to invade the kitchen regions, I might get some forth-right information from her.

This took some doing.

I cut more flowers than usual that morning for the vases and carried them all to the pantry. It was a small room with sinks and running water, the sides filled with shelves on which bowls and vases were neatly stored. It was at the end of a narrow corridor some distance from the kitchen quarters, and I could hear Cook singing cheerfully, if a trifle off key, as she clanked her pots and pans.

Rose should be putting the downstairs in order at this hour, while Kate would be doing the same above. Jock, I had seen grubbing in the flower beds on the entrance terrace, so there were only Mrs. Livingston and Vivian unaccounted for.

I tried humming to myself with increasing crescendo to attract Cook's attention, hoping that her normal Irish gregariousness would bring her to the pantry for a word. Her singing was, however, so much louder than mine that I doubt she heard me at all. Then a familiar tune caught my ear—the old and popular "Danny-Boy" and joining my voice with hers in the few words I could remember of the verse, I let out lustily. I heard her song die off, then heavy foot-steps were coming down the narrow passageway.

"Well, dear Heaven, listen to yourself now! A voice like a lark, it is, and yourself there as bright as the flowers you're fixin'!"

"Good morning, Delphia," I said cheerfully. "What delicious smells from the kitchen! Are you baking bread?"

A wide smile spread over her florid face. "Ah, shure 'tis the sweet smell of bakin' day that makes you so happy, then? Well, don't stand there makin' a hint. Come, and I'll give you a taste."

I followed her meekly to the kitchen, very much pleased with my clever little ruse.

The big room, although light and airy, was in the basement of the three-floored house, and its size staggered the imagination. One whole wall of stoves and ovens could easily accommodate the food for hundreds. On the other wall was a walk-in freezer and an enormous electric refrigerator. Cook opened this to take out fresh butter, and spreading it lavishly on a hot roll, she thrust it under my nose.

"Take a good, long sniff o' that. Sit yourself down now, and eat. There's nothin' like fresh-baked bread to water the mouth, is there?"

I sat down at the clean Formica-topped table and began to eat, while she lingered to absorb every nuance of praise. I grunted with animal pleasure, smiled up at her, and bit off another mouthful. She beamed at me. "Would y' like a cup o' tea to go with?"

"If you'll have one with me," I said.

When we were seated, I asked carelessly, "Where is everybody this beautiful morning? Where are Mrs. Livingston and Vivian?"

She raised her eyes to the ceiling and sniffed contemptuously, "The one's up there going over the accounts—and such a fuss it is, too! Save on this, save on that, 'til you'd think the wolf was at the very door, like. And the other's down there somewhere meetin' her lover, if I'm any judge."

"Vivian has a lover?" I almost choked. "Who is he?"

Cook shrugged. "Some no-good, no doubt. Niver a man of honor, you can be shure."

"Did you ever see him?"

"I mind my business," she said with great dignity. "But let thim be coming into my kitchen and there'll be trouble to pay."

Through the open door, I could see a clear access

to the upper part of the beach. A bit farther on, it was obscured from view.

"This is a pleasant place," I said. "You must enjoy looking out at the sea when you're sitting here with your tea."

"Sittin', she says," she echoed indignantly, "with the lot o' thim wantin' trays at all hours. It's Cook, would y' be after fixin' a pitcher of orange juice and a plate of cookies?" she said in a high, mincing tone in imitation of Mrs. Livingston at her most persuasive. "Or it's a wee sandwich and a pitcher of milk. If you ask me"—she leaned forward, her eyes wide with hidden knowledge—"it's snackin' in their own rooms they be. Oh, I see the crumbs, I do, whin I go to my own little hole up there under the eaves."

"But surely everyone here has more than enough to eat."

"Half me roast gone in the night!" she said loftily. "And beggars at the door wantin' a bite of this or that."

"You mean the monk?"

"It's no monk, that one is. A criminal, or worse, and Vivian—that fool girl—takin' him and his dirt right to the madam herself."

"He comes here to see Mrs. Regent?" I asked in profound disbelief.

Cook nodded importantly, pleased with herself for being the purveyor of gossip. "Right up those back steps, and sneaky as you please."

"But why? I've never seen him on the upper floor."

"And good reason. He comes in the night!" She tossed her head as though to absolve herself of all guilt in the matter. "Oh, I don't let on, mind you, but I hear one or the other of thim comin' down to un-latch me kitchen door. And let me tell you, that's there listenin' to me words, one day I'll let thim know I know."

"Why, this is outrageous," I said, trying to match my indignation to hers. "Surely Mrs. Regent doesn't want some 'beggar' interrupting her sleep?"

"Which is what I'm sayin', dearie. But they've got her, poor soul, under some evil spell, the three of thim. And before long—mark my words now—there'll be trouble to pay. He's that low, with his dressin' up like a good priest and deceivin' the good woman with his thievin', lyin' ways—"

"Did they ever say *why* he visits Mrs. Regent?"

"He makes her feel better."

An herb doctor, perhaps, I thought—and probably an imposter as well. I resolved to be on the lookout for him in the future. With Michael gone, and Annette lost to me, I was in a state of nerves.

Thinking of Annette brought me to the purpose of this invasion. I had finished three rolls and my tea, so I rose and asked casually, "By the way, have you ever seen a girl—very young and with copper-colored hair—down there on the beach?"

"Ah, the dear, blessed child—that I have!" Delphia touched her temple with a stubby finger. "Fey, poor darlin', and all of thim chasin' her outside and away to herself. Ah, the poor mite's a little angel if ever the good God made one. But fey, and shy as a deer, she is."

That was Annette all right, I thought. Warming to my task, I asked, "To whom does she belong? Where does she come from? Who is responsible for her?"

To my dismay, Delphia shrugged indifferently. "A waif, poor child. She was here when I came all of seven years ago—roamin' the place like a wild thing. Some wee waif from somewhere like the leprechauns brought her to play in the sun and the water."

"She has been here all those years?" I gasped. "Why on earth hasn't someone reported it to the authorities?"

"I mind my own business," Delphia said majestically, "until the right time comes." She rose with admirable stateliness and began to clear the table. "It's bad cess to a house that's divided," she said with quiet venom, "and it's God's way to punish the wicked and reward the just." This allegory seemed to close the discussion, but I was not ready to let her go.

"Have you seen the girl lately?" I asked intensely.

"She disappears from time to time—Heaven knows where to, poor mite."

"But when did you last see her?"

" 'Twas maybe a week or two, not more. She was runnin' to the house like all the divils was chasin' after her—that fast."

"Where does she sleep? Somewhere on the top floor? Maybe with the Livingstons?"

Delphia all but spat in indignation. "Thim three—they're all for thimselves and no other. No, she sleeps anywhere she takes a notion—that is, when she comes inside at all. She is a wild one, I'm sayin', and off like a deer at the first crack of dawn." She shook her head and sighed heavily. "Poor wee mite!"

I knew I couldn't get to the servants' quarters on the third floor without arousing suspicion, but I was convinced that something was terribly wrong with Annette. In order not to alarm Cook any further with my questions, I went back to the pantry after thanking her profusely for her hospitality. Although she had not given me the information I wanted about Annette, she did know of her existence, and so did the others. For some reason, the three Livingstons were keeping my darling Annette under wraps, her identity a secret. But why? Was she, as Charles had surmised, the child of Mrs. Regent's daughter, and because of her retardation, did they relegate her to the outdoors? I felt sure that Mrs. Regent wouldn't stand for this if she knew. In fact, hadn't she shown a curiosity about Annette one morning at breakfast? And hadn't Michael shown acute discomfort at the time? What *was* this conspiracy?

When my flowers were distributed to the various rooms, I went down to the beach, calling futilely, "Darling? Annette? Where are you, my pet? Come to Darling—come now!"

I might have continued longer had I not seen Vivian toiling along the upper slope from whatever rendezvous she had kept. I watched her out of sight—the ill-shaped figure, the unkempt clothes and hair, and wondered.

That night, I wrote to Charles, telling him of the deepening mystery and Annette's disappearance. "She always came to me when I called," I wrote through tear-blurred eyes. "Oh, she was so sweet and trusting with me, so distrustful of strangers. I miss her so, Charles—the games we shared and all her loveliness. I'm heartsick. I don't know what to do. Michael Davidson is to be gone some weeks, and I can't take this problem to Mrs. Regent. What shall I do? Cook says that trays go upstairs. They must be for Annette."

I wrote much more, telling him of the night visits of the robed man, of Vivian's alliance with someone —everything except Mrs. Regent's attempt at playing Cupid. That I couldn't bring myself to relate. It was too personal—too utterly ridiculous. I was folding the letter for the envelope when I heard a faint stirring in the next room, followed by low, furtive voices.

It was long after Mrs. Regent's bedtime and I had sat with her while she drank her hot milk. She had talked herself tired about the days of her European triumphs, promising soon to show me her accumulation of clippings, most of which she had put into albums when her hands were useful.

"We'll go to the music room and go through them all again," she had said eagerly. "And you shall paste them in for me. Someday perhaps someone will treasure them—Michael's wife or his children."

Unwilling to get off on this painful subject, I arranged her pillows and gave her an affectionate good night. When I was at the door, she called my name, and I came back into the room to hear what she was saying. "I'm so tired—so very tired. Tonight—I can sleep—"

I would have offered to get her an aspirin or a sleeping pill, but she was already gone.

And now there were voices in her rooms!

I crept close to the partition and listened. She seemed to be remonstrating drowsily to someone. But how had she got out of bed? Someone answered, and I felt relief when I recognized Vivian's voice, although I could not distinguish the words. There was a comparatively long silence, then movement, which sounded like Vivian's shuffling feet. Silence followed. I waited for some time before going into the hall. Vivian would have seen my light under the door, and surely she would have called me if anything were the matter. I made my way in the half-light to Mrs. Regent's door. There was no light, no sound. I made a resolution to ask her for a key to the connecting door between our rooms. It was I, not Vivian, who should be attending her needs in the middle of the night. That was why I had been placed here, wasn't it? And Michael Davidson depended on me.

CHAPTER 8

I had no reply to my letter to Charles. Two weeks passed, and although I queried Jock each time he brought up the mail, he merely handed me the bundle as though to say, "Go through it yourself." Jock seemed to be increasingly antagonistic toward me, which, in my state of frayed nerves, preyed upon my mind.

There was a noticeable failing in Mrs. Regent's health, too. Many mornings she did not feel well enough to have me join her for breakfast and, according to Vivian, had not slept well.

"Then I must see her," I said vigorously when the first of these messages came. "I am her nurse and I must decide if she needs a doctor."

Vivian planted her badly shod feet stubbornly in my doorway. "Mrs. Regent said to tell you that she will call you when she wants you."

Well, that's plain enough, I thought, sitting alone at breakfast downstairs and, as usual, scanning the beach for some sign of Annette. But there was nothing, no movement among the tar weed and pampas. She could have slipped into the water and been washed out to sea, my darling Annette. Even I was surprised at my love for her, and my grief. What would it be to see her running down the beach, carefree and well? I played with my food, wondering what to do with myself while I waited for Mrs. Regent's summons. If only Charles would write—or Michael return.

Somehow, in retrospect, Michael had taken on new and admirable qualities. His kindness to Mrs. Regent, his gentleness and grace in handling her and making her to seem less of an invalid, his concern for her. All of these showed a great deal of patience and deep devotion. I thought that now I wouldn't hesitate to tell him that I knew of Annette, and to ask him why, as manager of the estate, he allowed the girl to go hungry and uncared for. He knew that Annette lived precariously on the premises. Why hadn't he done something about it? This question made his admirable qualities sink somewhat in my estimation.

I felt frustrated and miserable. If it had not been for listening ears overhearing, I would have called Charles at his office and asked him to come. To unburden myself to him would have relieved me enormously. To add to my disconsolate state, the fog had crept in and was shrouding the beach and the windows in thick white, completely impenetrable. There was nothing for me to do, so I went to my own rooms to occupy myself with personal chores. I would launder a few things, then shampoo my hair and sit before the fire.

There was no fire in my sitting room, no sound anywhere of the maids cleaning. My bed was not made up, so I tended to it myself and set about straightening things. If Mrs. Regent didn't call me by noon, I would have the afternoon to roam the beach and look for Annette. It struck me that the fog would cover my movements in case Mrs. Livingston had become suspicious at my inquiry and was watching me.

After I had washed and towel-dried my hair, I paced the room restlessly, unable to settle down to anything. Perhaps Annette was somewhere in the vast complex of rooms, ill and feverish. Otherwise, for whom would the trays be fixed? Orange juice and cookies—fare for someone suffering from flu or a cold. I felt a wild surge of hope. Yes, that was it! She had never taken proper care of herself, running about barefoot in the surf and half-clad. She was sick. I gathered up a few pills—antihistamine, aspirin for the fever, and a mild sleeping potion. It was past noon and I wouldn't be needed until much later if Mrs. Regent felt like coming downstairs for dinner. I could prowl the various wings to my heart's content until I found my poor darling. After all, hadn't Mrs. Regent told me to feel free to go wherever I wished?

There was no one in the corridors, and everything was quiet. I ventured in the direction from which Michael had emerged one morning, quietly opening doors and closing them behind me. The other bedrooms were not nearly as elegant as my quarters, I noticed. Once I came upon a masculine room smelling of pipe tobacco and assumed that this must be Michael's. It was untidy, books and papers scattered over the desk, but fascinating for all that. Bolder now, I pored over the papers without touching them, noting the scribbled figures on the top page. Accounts, no doubt. I wondered again why Michael and Mrs. Livingston stressed economy so firmly when Mrs. Regent had said that Michael would one day be a very rich man as her heir. There seemed to be contradictions on every hand.

I was about to give up my search and take a walk when I came to a pair of heavily carved double doors. Estimating the layout of the house, this must be Mrs. Regent's music salon and directly over her suite. My heart quickening, I tried the doors and found they yielded.

The long room was darkened, the draperies drawn over the windows. In the dimness, I could see a concert grand piano, and I touched it gingerly, saddened that its dulcet tones were stilled long since. The furniture was shrouded, although a certain smell of wax gave the impression of regular cleaning. Shelves were crowded with sheet music, tape recordings and albums. It was very still.

I examined the shelves and cabinets, finding my way in the half-light until I came upon a glass-encased piece of furniture filled with easel photographs. Curiously, I opened it. One full-length picture was of Mrs. Regent in a ball gown, a jeweled coronet on her hair. How beautiful the supple figure, slim and well-proportioned! How lovely the hands, not yet knotted and gnarled with arthritis! I took the picture to the window and pulled back the draperies to see it better, struck with a vague familiarity.

Why, I thought in sudden choking discovery, *she looks like Annette!*

Impetuously, I returned to the cabinet to look at the other photographs. Most of them were of Mrs. Regent, stately and tall in her lovely gowns and flashing jewels, but there was one of a laughing young lady of, perhaps, twenty. Sylvia? I found others, noting the resemblance to her mother in face and form. And then, to end all my doubts, a picture of them together, Mrs. Regent and Sylvia, their arms entwined in deep affection. "Annette!" I said aloud. "She looks exactly like Annette. *She* is her mother!"

I put the photographs back carefully and closed the glass doors. So this was where Mrs. Regent kept all the treasures of the past, in her beloved music room! And Annette *was* her own grandchild! I was as sure of it as though she had told me herself.

I turned to go when, in a corner, I saw something

that made me freeze. There was a sleeping bag and a pile of blankets! This must be where Annette slept. But something told me that she had not been here for some time. A flimsy nightgown, worn from many washings, was flung near the pile of bedding. Yes, this was Annette's lodging!

Excited by my discovery, and disappointed, too, that she was not here, I ran back to my room for a warm coat and scarf. Cook had said that she often disappeared and slept no one knew where. She might have another sleeping bag and have made herself a little place of her own along the beach in some undiscovered cove. Under cover of the fog, I could investigate thoroughly.

I heard nothing, saw no one downstairs. I had forgotten lunch and was hungry, but that would have to wait. This, I felt, was my day to find Annette and, please God, she would be well and as mischievous as ever.

I must have prowled for hours, going into the wilder part where stones, boulders, and scrub growth impeded my progress as my stout shoes stumbled over fallen branches and sunk into damp pits. The fog was so thick that I had the sensation of being lost as I groped about, searching for a cove where my little fawn might be hiding. Finally, I reached out in the thickness and touched something—the cyclone fence. I breathed with relief. At least I could orient myself by following the fence to the place where we had seen the trailer, then bear directly toward the promontory and Regent Manor.

I crept along slowly, feeling with my torn and soiled fingers. The fog had brought an early darkness, and in the distance I could hear the sea boiling angrily. My hand caught at a splinter, and I withdrew it quickly, sucking at the place uncomfortably; then I saw that it was the knothole through which Annette had shown me the trailer house. I peeked through, trying to accustom my eyes to the swirling fog. I saw the outline of the trailer, grim and deserted and without light. Nothing there. But I had my directions now and, hungry, wet, and tired, I headed toward the comforts of home, a fire and tea.

I had taken only a few steps when I heard a sound, soft and cushioned by the fog. I stopped to listen, calling softly, "Who is it? Annette, is that you?"

It came again, a mewing of misery such as I had heard that first night when Annette crouched at my door. I felt along the fence, my foot frantically searching for the flat stone that Annette had climbed to scale the fence.

"I'm coming, darling!" I shouted, heedless of who might hear. "I'm coming." The mewing sound came again and again, but muffled as though my little kitten might be gagged. Fear for her tore at me, leaving me breathless. I found the stone, slippery with moss, and steadied my feet on its precarious tip. It was still some distance to the top of the fence, but I could make it unless I slipped. I gripped the top with my hands, and laboriously brought my body high enough to see over the top; then, dragging myself up without foothold, I was astraddle the fence and letting myself down on the other side.

There was no light inside the trailer, but I approached cautiously all the same. Annette's crying had increased in intensity, and it sounded as though she were trying to mouth words through a thick bandage over her mouth. Thoroughly frightened now, I crept past the long side of the trailer, bending to avoid discovery from the windows, and found the door. What evil awaited inside? Why would the squat man imprison the girl? Was he angry at her trespassing and determined to teach her a cruel lesson by leaving her here, bound and alone? I tried the door after assuring myself that there was no car nearby, and it opened with a chilling creak of hinges.

The small living room was empty, with the kitchen in plain view and also empty. A brown robe hung lifelessly on a peg. *The monk!*

Terror gripped me anew. "Annette!" I screamed into the stillness. "Where are you?"

There was the sound of a lurching body hurling itself about and striking something. The gagging sounds were awful. I opened another door and found her!

My first impression was one of unmitigated horror. Annette's hair was matted and falling over her face, the wild eyes peering through, and on her hands and feet I saw manacles!

"Oh, darling! How am I ever going to get you loose?"

She struggled wildly, trying to speak, and I stooped to rip the tape from her mouth and pull the wadding from it. At first, she seemed unable to find her voice, then she emitted a weak croak that sounded like a garbled "Darling!"

I found a switch and snapped on the ceiling light, one dim bulb. I was babbling as hysterically as Annette, talking to myself and to her. "I must get these chains off, but how? Annette, my sweet, how did he fasten them? With a key?"

She nodded, her blue eyes enormous. I had no time to find a small thing like a key. I ran to the kitchen and rifled through the cabinet drawers for a knife, a file—anything. By now, all the lights were on and I felt eerily conscious of my plight and hers. If the man returned, we could never escape. I found a screwdriver and tackled the wristbands tightly bind-

ing her hands. The bands were of some thin, strong
stuff, not iron—maybe aluminum—and I pried clumsily, gouging the slender little wrists but evoking no
cry, until I had them loose enough for her to slip her
hands out. Next the anklets. These took longer.

"All right, now, darling—another minute and we'll
be well away from here. Pull, dear, hard! There, you
see? Now the other— Hold still, sweet, until I get it
loosened."

When she was free, both of us stood looking down
at the cruel contraption. He had bound her like a
helpless animal, the beast! On the way out, I snatched
the offensive brown robe to wrap her in against the
cold.

The lights were out, the door snugly closed, and
we were breathing the blessed damp air when Annette grabbed my wrist and pointed. Two wisps of
light were skimming the horizon, arcs against the sky
—a car!

"Quick," she croaked. "To the bushes."

She led the way, her bare feet soundless and my
own crackling through the underbrush with frighten-
ing noise. The car was coming closer, the sound of
the motor rumbling through the muffle of fog.
Where would those merciless headlights focus? Annette seemed to have no fear—only a fervid determination to escape. We dropped down beside the
fence, and I pulled the brown robe over our huddled bodies.

"I'm hungry," Annette whimpered hoarsely.

"Sh! Don't move, and keep quiet!"

The car came closer, stopped with a grinding of
brakes, and a man got out. I could hear him moving
about, muttering to himself, and I risked a peek
through the robe. In the glare, he was lifting the hood
of the car and doing something inside, his head ob-

scured. When he emerged with an oath and straightened, I saw him plainly. He stood for a moment in wrathful perplexity, and the light caught his glasses —thick glasses—and on his face I saw the cruel lines with which I was familiar. I saw a boy dissecting a live frog! I held my breath in a superhuman effort to keep from screaming.

It was Clarence Gibbs!

Everything that I had ever known of Clarence Gibbs came back to me in those next terrifying moments. He had been a cruel, shrill, ugly little boy, meek and obsequious with those who were older and stronger, bullying and teasing and pulling the hair of those who were smaller and weaker. And, for some sadistic reason, I was regularly his victim. Had it not been for Matt and his brotherly watchfulness over me, I might have suffered worse fates than having snowballs rubbed in my face and dropped down my neck on the way home from school. Or having my tiny kitten tied up with strings of tin cans and set loose to literally kill herself in fright of the clatter. His slitted eyes behind the thick glasses gleamed with hate and malice at all times, except when they were discreetly lowered in the presence of authority.

For all his corruption, Clarence was smart, and he knew that in order to survive and perpetrate his cruelties, he needed to have the approval of his betters. Teachers praised and petted him, partly in pity for his grotesque appearance, partly in admiration of his intellect. Little did they suspect his foulness of speech and action. I wondered how much of this innate savagery he had inflicted on my precious Annette. I held her closer to me under the filthy brown robe that smelled of body and scalp odor.

The car lights were out now and Clarence was

stumbling around in the trailer, cursing and kicking at things, and obviously very drunk. Soon he would come outside to look for us, perhaps with a torch, and if this happened, I must be ready to hold him off while Annette escaped over the cyclone fence. I groped around in the darkness until I laid my hands upon a fairly ominous-sized stone. I spoke to Annette quickly:

"If he finds us when he comes out, you must run to the fence and go over without waiting. Otherwise, we'll remain very quietly until he gives up."

"No," she whimpered. "You come, too."

"I'll come later," I soothed, "after you are well over. Run straight back to the house as fast as you can. Now, do as I say!"

I regretted having to be so harsh with her but, having been so brave, she was now beginning to collapse.

An angry slam of the door told me that Clarence was outside. The headlights of the car were turned on and shone through the robe. Thank heaven, they were not trained directly on us! I held Annette's hands tightly in mine, waiting and praying, while Clarence plowed around in the underbrush near the trailer, mumbling and swearing. He would assume, perhaps, that the girl was alone, yet how could she have extricated herself from those manacles? I clutched the stone tightly. How long had he held her in captivity? I dared not think.

For some remote reason, he gave up the search fairly soon and went back inside. However, the lights still burned, and I felt it unsafe to move from our hiding place. If he heard anything, he might reappear —with a weapon. Annette was shivering against me with fear and shock.

I don't know how long we lay there, stiff and cold. An hour? Hours? There was no way of gauging the

time in this limitless fog. Annette dozed fitfully, cud-
dled close to me like a kitten. I could feel the soft
roundness of her young body, and the trust. The poor
child thought she was safe simply because I was there.
But I knew I must not underestimate Clarence Gibbs's
wily cleverness. Even when the trailer and the car
showed dark, I was afraid to reveal our whereabouts
by the slightest movement. It was like playing cat-
and-mouse with a leopard. I was cramped and stiff,
and terribly concerned about the half-clad girl beside
me. If I did not get her blood circulating soon, she
could be the victim of exposure.

I moved tentatively, tempting the pursuer to action. There was nothing. Growing bolder, I poked
my head out to look around, but visibility was too
poor to see anything.

Annette stirred. "Shall we go now? she whispered.

"Wait." I found a pebble and threw it. Nothing
happened. Maybe Clarence was so drunk he was
deeply asleep by now. In any case, our best bet was
to move soon. Softly, I whispered, "Do you think you
can find the fence?"

"Yes."

"Can you get over it?"

"Yes." Her patience and obedience in this emer-
gency was astounding.

"Then go very quietly. Try not to make a sound.
When you are safely over, I will come."

She crawled out from under the robe without hes-
itation. I watched her out of sight, which was only a
few feet in this encroaching mist, and listened. Not a
sound. Good girl, I thought, like an Indian. I heard a
faint crunch as she dropped into the bushes on the
other side of the fence.

Now it was my turn. I removed my walking shoes
and crept slowly toward the fence. Surely if Clarence

were awake, he would make some move about now. Cold chills danced up and down my spine. Step by step, I drew closer to the fence that meant safety, until I found the stone. There was some sound of my clothing scraping against the wood as I drew myself up to the top of the fence with all my strength, then the drop into the bushes.

I reached for Annette's hand and pulled the robe about her. "Now, run," I said. "And don't stop until we are home!"

CHAPTER 9

The rescue, spectacular as it was, was nothing in comparison to the problem of getting into the Manor once we reached it. The front door was locked and bolted, as I had known it would be. Dragging Annette along, I went to the terrace and tried the French doors. Locked! One by one, we tried the windows until, in her nocturnal knowledge of escape hatches, Annette said, "I think I know a way."

She was in full control now, leading me to the kitchen wing, both of us trying doors and windows as we went, until we reached the pantry corridor. "Sometimes I come in this way."

"Please be careful not to make any noise," I whispered. Annette's life might still be in danger, even in this house, from her enemies. Why would anyone wish to harm her? That was a question that would have to wait. But, one thing sure, I'd have the police on Clarence Gibbs early tomorrow morning! Kidnapping was a Federal offense and punishable by death. The "faith healer" had gone too far this time.

The creaky old door yielded, and we were in the dry warmth of the flower pantry. From there, we felt our way along the walls to the kitchen. The smells of cold food assailed us, and Annette cried pitifully, "I'm hungry!"

I kept her close to me while I rummaged about the

unfamiliar place for bread. There would be meat and milk in the refrigerator, and, still in mortal fear of discovery, I found an end of veal and took a carton of milk. This would ease our hunger until morning, and, meantime, I must think what to do with my charge. What, I wondered, had they thought of my absence at dinner? It seemed eons ago that I had set out on my walk this afternoon.

We crept up the back stairs without mishap and were safely in my rooms, where the heat of the furnace still lingered. I stripped off Annette's wet clothes and dried her slim young body tenderly. Well wrapped in the extra blankets, I watched her claw at the meat and bread, washing down each mouthful with huge draughts of milk. I undressed and joined her in the welcome feast. Aside from being dirty, her hair matted into knots, Annette looked quite well. Her appetite was as ravenous as ever, her color good. I wanted to know so many things, but this was not the time for questions. She had been bound to the bed in the trailer but unable to lie upon it. She must be dead tired. When she had finished eating, I tucked her into my own bed and climbed in beside her. Dazed by food and comfort, she had nothing to say and, except for cuddling close to me and drawing my arm over her body, she scarcely moved again.

I, however, lay awake for hours. The robe, I thought suddenly—where was it? On the kitchen floor where Annette had dropped it while we were foraging for food? Well, what matter? I suppressed a wry smile, thinking that Delphia would probably have a wild Irish fit on finding it there. Let them *be* implicated, the Livingstons! It was about time some facts came to the fore. A girl whom I loved as dearly as though she were my own had been held captive by a man I knew to be a monster, and I meant to take action.

But the more I thought in this vein, the more I knew it to be impractical. Someone was in this with Gibbs, and Annette was not yet free from danger. But who? Vivian? I saw again her return to the house along the promontory. Had she been visiting Gibbs? Was he the "lover" who had turned her head? He was also the monk with the flowing false beard and hair. He probably had a dozen different disguises. But why would he want to hold Annette captive? For money? Who in this house had any money, except Mrs. Regent? And she didn't even know of Annette's existence. "She had no children," she had said of Sylvia. But I knew now that Annette was Sylvia's child and the grandchild of the matriarch whom everyone had gone to such pains to deceive.

Where did Michael fit into all this? Had Sylvia died giving birth to this retarded girl? Why, when Annette would have been such a comfort to Mrs. Regent, had Michael Davidson chosen to keep her birth a secret for fourteen years? Oh yes, this was a tough nut to crack, one that required a far more analytical mind than I possessed.

One thing sure: I must trust no one! Delphia or Charles might have been acceptable under ordinary circumstances, but Delphia was ridden with hate for the Livingstons, which made her undependable at present, and someone had cut off all communication between Charles and me. Jock? He seemed the logical one; he had charge of the mail and could secrete a letter at will.

My whirling mind brought me back to the one immediate question: what was I going to do with Annette? I must keep her hidden. But how? Kate did the upstairs rooms, and she would think it strange if I asked her to pass over mine. And there was someone in this house who had entered my rooms with a pass-key and gone through my belongings! No, Annette would not be safe here for any length of time. Then, where?

I suddenly remembered the huddle of blankets in the music room. Apparently, she had slept there at one time. But the maids would be cleaning there on occasion, discover her, and raise an alarm. Of the fifty or so rooms in this house, was there no hiding place?

Finally, I drifted off to sleep from sheer exhaustion.

A dull rain had supplanted the fog by morning. It dripped dismally from the eaves and splattered against the windows with staccato persistence. I groped for the bedside clock and saw that it was nearly nine o'clock. Vivian would be knocking at my door any moment to summon me to Mrs. Regent's suite for breakfast. I tucked the covers closely about Annette and fled to the bathroom for my shower. Everything must appear to be perfectly normal to the prying, hostile eyes of Vivian.

By the time I had dressed in a warm wool sheath, I heard stirrings and faint murmurings from Mrs. Regent's suite. I shook Annette awake and cautioned her to slip the door bolt after me and neither speak nor let anyone in except me.

"I'll knock four times," I said. "One, two, three, four—understand?"

Shortly, Vivian's knock came, and I closed the door to my bedroom and greeted her with a cheery good morning. Apparently, there was nothing amiss so far as she was concerned, for she was the same as usual.

"Mrs. Regent wants you to have breakfast with her." Then she added with some show of authority, "But don't tire her. She isn't well."

"Then why hasn't her doctor been called?" I challenged, knowing full well that the "doctor" was Clarence Gibbs dressed in the regalia of a mendicant monk. "I'm sorry, but I shall have to take charge here and see that my patient has the proper medication."

Some perturbation showed on the surly features before Vivian said, "All right, I'll see what can be done. I'll try to get a message to him sometime today."

"Why not use the telephone? He has offices, doesn't he? What is his name?"

All this was too direct for the deceitful woman. "His name is Raphael," she said, and walked away. I waited to see that she didn't linger near my rooms.

I went into Mrs. Regent's rooms rather pleased with myself. "Raphael" was the name BJ had said Clarence Gibbs used for his faith healing. I dared him to come here and confront me! I hoped he would! I could imagine his dismay when he was unmasked. Not that I would consider doing anything to upset Mrs. Regent. But if she needed real medical attention, I was determined to see that she got it. And, oh, I did relish the prospect of seeing that creepy little Clarence Gibbs's face when he saw me!

My patient was sitting up in bed, with mounds of tiny pillows stacked around her, lovely as always in her pretty pink bedjacket and finely woven coverlets. Her eyes, though, were not as bright, and I suspected increased pain when she lifted her cup with an effort.

"I have missed you," I said when greetings were over and I was seated with my own breakfast. "I waited until noon to see you yesterday, then took a walk."

"Oh, isn't it a miserable day?" she wailed. "My arthritis is always so much worse in damp weather, and I'm afraid we're in for a stretch of it. Do you like your kippers? I thought they might be a change."

"Delicious," I said, eating the first hot meal I had had in twenty-four hours. I wondered if she would ask me where I had been last night, so I decided to fabricate something to forestall the question. "Charles was in the area yesterday, and he stopped to take me for a ride. You were resting, so I didn't disturb you."

She forced a wan smile, not much caring, I thought. "Don't be concerned in the least, my dear. The Livingstons had urgent business in the village and left Kate to watch over me. I'm afraid that things don't go too well when Mrs. Livingston is absent. Was your dinner all right?"

"I sort of foraged for myself," I said in all truth. "You mustn't worry about me. But I do about you, you know. Won't you let me get you something for the pain until the doctor comes?"

She raised herself on the pillows with some show of distress. "Oh, no! Don't tell me Dr. Raphael is coming again tonight? I told Vivian not to—"

"I'm the one responsible," I quickly interjected. "When Vivian told me how poorly you've been, I suggested that he be summoned."

"Oh dear! I do wish you hadn't, Marly. I really do not wish to see him."

"Then he was here last night?"

"Yes, he was," she said with absolute frankness. "And I don't like his new treatment at all. Faith is one thing, and I was doing very well by following his suggestions for thought-control. But these herb concoctions he has put me on are so—sickening!" She gestured toward her midriff delicately. "I can't seem to keep anything down. My entire system rebels."

"Then let us have another opinion, Mrs. Regent. That is quite a common practice in medicine, you know, and I'm sure that your Dr. Raphael would see the advantages of a consultation with one or more other physicians."

For a moment something like hope dawned in her eyes, then she shook her head slowly. "No, it would never do," she said positively. "Vivian would oppose it, even if the doctor consented. She has been very cross with me lately for fussing about the herbs—such nasty stuff." She looked at me as though measuring my sincerity, then said, "When one is helpless, as I am, one knows the importance of keeping the household climate harmonious. The Livingstons are probably the only people in the world who would have sacrificed their own lives entirely in deference to my needs—the only ones. I am completely dependent on them, and especially on Vivian, for my well-being."

I placed my cup in the saucer with a clink. "You are the mistress of this household, Mrs. Regent. *Your* wishes are paramount, not Vivian's."

"You—just—don't—understand," she said sorrowfully. "I don't expect you to. No one could, even Michael."

Michael's name gave me fresh courage to push my point. "Mr. Davidson put you in *my* care before he went away. I should feel remiss in his trust, and in my duties as a nurse, if I allowed this to continue when it is so apparently detrimental to your health."

"I know, I know! I can see your side of it, too. But don't you see? There is no one to take care of me if I offend Vivian and her parents?"

"I am here for that express purpose," I reminded her. "I am a nurse, engaged by Michael Davidson to care for your health, not to do flower arrangements and write letters for you. I must, in loyalty to him and to you, see that you have the best medical care."

I saw that she was disturbed, and tempted, too, to

put her problems in my hands. She plucked at the coverlet in agitation, a trait that I had never known her to exhibit before. She had always seemed so calm, so confident and cheerful. Now she was an old lady bereft of friends.

"I can't," she said after a few moments. "Please don't ask me, for I simply cannot. There are reasons of long-standing, and of which you have no knowledge."

She was so disturbed that I changed the subject at once. Besides, I was beginning to worry about Annette in the adjoining rooms. If she became impatient at my delay, she might do all sorts of things to attract someone. Her attention span was so limited that she might already have forgotten my instructions. After all, she needed me and must be my first consideration until I had her safely hidden from those who would harm her.

"I mustn't tire you further, Mrs. Regent. If there is anything I can do for you, you have only to let me know."

"Thank you, my dear. It is a comfort to have you here."

"And Michael will be returning before long," I said with a smile. "That will be a tonic better than medicine for you."

She responded at once with a smile that was both hopeful and sad. "I wish he were here now."

"Then let me put in a call for him," I said eagerly. "I'm sure he'd come at once."

"No. No, this lecture series means too much to him. I have never been able to bring myself to interfere in the lives of those I love."

"Then will you have Vivian notify me when Dr. Raphael comes?"

Again the reluctance in her face. I felt sorry to harass her with my demands, but I could not allow that quack and Vivian to sicken her in this evil way any longer. Were they trying to kill her with poisonous drugs during this interim when Michael was not near to protect her? Something wicked was in the air, some devious trick to harm her in mind, in body, and render her incompetent. I waited for her answer.

"I'll see what is best," she more or less agreed finally. "I appreciate your concern, dear. It's just that I am bound to—others."

I was obliged to be content with that. Everything must appear to be normal and undisturbed to Vivian, her parents, and Clarence Gibbs. Otherwise, they might move in violence before I could get Annette to safety. And that was of prime importance. I half-expected Vivian to be huddled near the door, but she was nowhere in sight. Had she gone to Clarence? And what would be her reaction when he told her that Annette had been rescued? Kate was coming down the hall, and I intercepted her.

"Would you mind letting my rooms go for a day or two, Kate?" I tried to think of some excuse and came up with a very thin one. "I—am writing a book and—I'd rather not be disturbed."

"A book?" she said in some excitement, her peasant mind doubting nothing. "My goodness! I never knew anyone who could write a book before. What is it about? Can I read it?"

I couldn't have hoped for a more ardent response. "I'm only just starting it, Kate," I lied gently, "but if it's ever published, I shall see that you have the first copy if you'll preserve my privacy."

"Oh, I will, I will, Miss Carewe! Can I get you anything? A typewriter—some paper or pencils. There's lots of old stuff in the storerooms downstairs."

It was all so easy now that I had embarked on a

path of lies and deceit. And if it was this easy for me, think how those professional liars had been able to throw this entire household off the scent of their schemes to harm Mrs. Regent and Annette!

"I shall not need anything at present," I said, "but when I do, Kate, I'll call on you for help. And would you please not say anything to the others about this?" I knew that the staff would be notified immediately and this, I thought, would account for my being remote in the days to come. She watched me curiously for a moment, then went about her duties. I had a chance to tap on my door four times.

Annette slid the bolt. I slipped in quietly, and stopped short in amazement, all my fears realized.

The child was burning up with fever!

CHAPTER 10

Two very sick patients, and not a friend in sight!

That's exactly what my predicament amounted to in the next week.

Under Vivian's care and the "herbs" with which she plied Mrs. Regent, that poor lady was now unable to retain food or liquids. She was gradually wasting away into nothingness, barely able to speak, her mind wandering much of the time.

My own little Annette had responded somewhat to antihistamine, until a vicious cough had taken hold, and now I was afraid of pneumonia. I was desperate in my need.

Although food was the least of our wants in the present crisis, I waylaid the impressionable Kate one early morning and, pressing a generous bill into her hand, said, "Kate, I need two things at once: the key to the door between mine and Mrs. Regent's rooms, and plenty of milk and fruit juices, hot tea regularly, and whatever else you can manage without anyone's knowing. I will pay you and Rose double this if you will help me to get Mrs. Regent well."

I had put on my nurse's uniform that morning, and it may have been the authority that it signified, the sight of my strained face, or the desperation in my voice, but Kate readily agreed to oblige. She brought me the key almost immediately.

"Please don't let on to Mrs. Livingston," she begged, "or Vivian. Rose and I would lose our positions here if they knew."

I assured her that no one would be informed, then I went inside, opened the suites, and shot the sturdy bolts on each of the sitting-room doors. There was no other means of access.

That was a dreadful day, with Vivian knocking all day long and threatening me with dire results if I didn't let her in. Fortunately, both patients were only half-conscious and hardly roused at the continuous argument and knocking. I bathed Annette almost constantly in an effort to bring down her fever. Mrs. Regent, I gave emetics from my medical store to cause her to vomit the poison in her system. By late night, when the household had retired and left me alone, I found a tray outside my door with provisions that would do for my patients' nourishment for several days.

And I had another inspiration. I could use the only telephone in the house. It was enclosed in a booth underneath the stairway. I took my cigarette lighter in order to see the directory and dialed the first physician whose name I came to, a Dr. Alden.

It was nearly midnight, and I could tell by his voice that he had been in bed.

"Dr. Alden, this is Miss Carewe. I am a nurse employed to care for Mrs. Regent at the Manor, and I need you at once."

"Regent Manor?" he said in surprise. "Nobody is allowed to go there."

"That's right," I said. "But my patient has been under the care of a quack, and I have reason to believe that she is suffering from fairly mild doses of arsenic administered often in small amounts and which she believes to be 'herbs.'"

"Symptoms, Miss Carewe?"

I liked his professional approach. "Vertigo, dizziness—a rather noticeable skin rash appeared today."

"Vomiting?"

"Yes, but I gave her an emetic to clear her stomach. After that, she was able to retain some milk."

There was a moment's pause before he asked, "How do I get in?"

Time was passing and I might be discovered at any moment. I spoke fast. "Above the property at the skyline there is a cyclone fence, Doctor. Avoid attracting any attention from the occupant of the trailer there, but bring a flashlight and come directly south to the promontory. It leads to the back of the house. I dare not turn on any lights, but I will leave the kitchen door open and meet you there."

"I'll be with you in twenty minutes," he said briskly, and hung up.

I had forgotten to ask him to bring *terramyacin* for Annette! Praying that he would have it in his medical kit, I stole quietly through the house and down to the kitchen to unbolt the door. I had had little sleep these past days and my nerves were screaming. But once the doctor was here, I thought, there would be an end to my problems. I could tell him about "Dr. Raphael," and he would notify the authorities.

It seemed an eternity until I saw a small, squat figure in dark trousers and mackintosh picking his way down the hill toward the house. For a moment, I crouched behind the door, fearful that it might be Clarence. Then he was by my side, speaking very low, and I was guiding him up the back stairway to the hall above.

Some prickle of apprehension crawled along my senses when we reached the open corridor above.

Running ahead of Dr. Alden to the front of the house, I saw that Mrs. Regent's door, which I had been obliged to leave unlocked, but closed, was hanging open. A sliver of light lay upon the carpet, and I rushed in anticipating I knew not what.

Vivian was standing over Mrs. Regent's bed, her face constricted, her hands clenched. She looked up at my entrance, her eyes livid with hatred.

"What have you done to my lady?" she cried, lunging for me. "What did you give her?"

Her eyes widened when Dr. Alden followed me into the room, and she backed away.

"Vivian," I said, "I want you to tell the doctor exactly what you have been giving Mrs. Regent." She retreated several more steps, and I caught hold of her, shaking her by the shoulders. "Tell him, Vivian, or you'll be responsible for—whatever happens."

"You're the nurse," she said accusingly, her mouth slack with fear. "Whatever happens to her, *you* did it! You locked me out and poisoned her."

The doctor had pulled back the bedclothes and was listening to Mrs. Regent's heartbeat with his stethoscope. "Get that woman out of here," he said, "and keep her out!"

I pushed Vivian through the door and bolted it. Thank heaven she had not discovered Annette. What would she do? Raise the household?

Mrs. Regent was moaning now, and I went to her side so that she wouldn't be confused at the sight of a stranger bending over her.

"This is Dr. Alden, Mrs. Regent. He has come to help you."

"Oh, Marly, you shouldn't have!" she said weakly before the doctor thrust a thermometer into her mouth.

He examined the sores on her body and said, "Arsenic poisoning all right." He was preparing a hypodermic. "I'm going to give her three milligrams of dimercaprol—to be followed regularly every four to six hours. You called me just in time, Nurse. Another day would have been too late."

Mrs. Regent winced as the needle went into her arm. I took the thermometer from her mouth, and she said, "I'm so dizzy, Marly."

The doctor pulled a chair up to her bed and started to massage the area where the needle had been. "Mrs. Regent, have you any idea who might want to harm you?"

She shook her head. "I have left them all provided for in my will. Why should any of them want to harm me?"

The doctor's heavy brows lifted at me in a mute verification of my own suspicions. "I'm going to give you something to make you sleep comfortably, Mrs. Regent. I'll leave capsules for your pain with Miss Carewe. But don't take anything from anyone but her —understand?"

"This—is—all—so—sordid," I heard her say before her eyes closed.

The doctor shut his bag and nodded for me to follow him into the sitting room.

"Are her servants trying to kill her?" he asked bluntly.

"Doctor, there is another patient," I said hastily. "Pneumonia."

"For Heaven's sake, girl, why didn't you say so? Where is she?"

Annette looked like an animated doll tossing in the bed, her cheeks pink and the long lashes fanning her face.

"Exposure," I said. "She had been responding to antihistamine until the lung congestion set in."

"How long ago?"

"Nearly a week."

"Great Scott!" he exclaimed impatiently. "You do expect miracles, don't you?"

"I'll explain that—later. Let me awaken her, Doctor. She is afraid of strangers."

Annette opened her eyes at my touch, looking around the room in apparent fright while she oriented herself. "Darling!" she whispered through parched lips. "Water."

"Annette, I have brought someone to help you."

She shrank into a pitiful huddle as she saw the doctor. "No, no! Go away!"

I admired the way Dr. Alden spoke gently as he approached the bed. "Annette, is it? What a pretty girl! You've been very sick, Annette, but I'm a doctor and I'm going to give you something to make you well. Have you ever had a shot?"

In spite of her aversion to anyone she did not know, I could see that Annette was beginning to relax. "Shot?" she asked. "Like a gun?"

"No, not like a gun, Annette. More like a pin prick." He rolled up her sleeve and showed her the upper arm. "It will hurt a little, but only for a moment."

He had prepared the hypodermic and was sponging the arm with cotton when the clatter outside Mrs. Regent's rooms began. Jock was pounding on the door, his voice demanding entrance. Behind him, I could hear the voices of Mrs. Livingston and Vivian. Annette stiffened.

"Make them let you in, Dad," Vivian shrieked.

"Break the door down, Jock, if you have to."

The doctor plunged the needle into Annette's arm under cover of the commotion, and she scarcely seemed to feel it. He rubbed it carefully and then strode to the door.

"You people are disturbing my patients," he said with considerable authority, "and I'll have you held accountable. Now go away and be quiet."

"What are you doing to her?" Mrs. Livingston said.

"Trying to counteract the poison that some fiend has given her and—" He would have mentioned Annette if I had not hushed him. "Now go away and don't come back."

"She has her own doctor."

"Then get him here at once. There are a few things I'd like to ask him."

The clamor subsided, and I heard them whispering together before they retreated.

"I don't think I can get you out for awhile, Doctor," I said apologetically. "I'm afraid that you've become a prisoner like I am—and the patients."

"Don't worry about it," he said comfortably, going back to check Annette again. "My family knows where I am, and if I'm not back by morning, there'll be the devil to pay. What's it all about, anyway? Do you care to tell me?"

Annette was drifting off into a more normal sleep, so I took him into my sitting room. How stolid and comforting he was as I poured forth the lurid tale—kidnapping and suspicion of attempted murder. I could hardly believe it myself as I related it in a shaking voice. He listened attentively, interjecting a question occasionally. To me, he seemed like the Rock of Gibraltar.

"I always heard this was a peculiar establishment," he said slowly when I had finished. "Who is the girl?"

"I have reason to believe that she is Mrs. Regent's granddaughter. But Mrs. Regent does not know of her existence."

"All these years here, and Mrs. Regent has never seen her?" he asked incredulously. "This is like something out of the Arabian Nights—a phantasy!"

"You must remember that Mrs. Regent has been almost completely helpless for many years."

His stubby fingers felt his jaw, making a scratching sound. "And until you came into the picture no one ever thought to ask any questions—that it? What about this Michael you mentioned. He in on it, too?"

I hesitated to implicate Michael in so many words. "I— No, I don't think so."

"But he's able-bodied. He must have seen the girl —been aware of her existence. Why would he keep her identity from her grandmother?"

"Only one reason that I can think of, Doctor. You probably noticed that Annette is slightly retarded."

"No wonder, if she's been roaming the wilds for fourteen years. Good Lord! She probably hasn't been to school—can't read or write. No, Nurse, I disagree with you on any signs of retardation. It's only a lack of opportunity to live normally that has made her shy and peculiar." He slapped his knee. "What do you know? Isn't this a mystery to end them all? You can write a book when you get out of this."

"If I ever do," I said pensively. "Doctor, what shall I do now? Or rather, when Mrs. Regent and Annette are well?"

"Well-ll," he said thoughtfully, "let's think about this now. Do you have any friends?"

"Only Charles Christian in San Francisco. He mistrusted this case from the beginning, and for a while we kept in touch. But I think Jock put a stop to that. I didn't make any accusations, you see, because Annette was missing and I had to find her. Until today, when I locked the doors up here, no one suspected me of knowing."

"Cat's out of the bag now, though. And from what

I heard, that Vivian is ready to throw you to the lions."

"For poisoning Mrs. Regent, yes. She wouldn't hesitate if the chips were down."

"Uh-huh. You say the faith healer lives in the trailer? Pretty low character, is he?"

"Abominable. I knew him at home in Kansas, but I didn't make the connection until I rescued Annette. Then I recognized him."

"What did he want with her? Do you suppose she was getting troublesome and they wanted him to take her away and—well, just drop her somewhere, the way some people do a cat or dog they don't want anymore?"

"Or kill her," I said with a shiver. "He's capable of anything."

"Money in it somewhere. They don't want Mrs. Regent to know, or the girl would be the heiress. Still, I've always heard that she didn't have much. I know for a fact that she's been selling off land here. This place used to be twice the size it is now. What does your Michael have to say about that?"

I thought that question over for a moment before answering. For some reason, I wanted to protect Michael. He was kind to Mrs. Regent and, I was convinced, sincerely devoted to her. Still, I had heard her reproving him for selling a parcel of land. And she had also teased him about her accounts and calling her extravagant.

"Mrs. Regent thinks she is rich," I said, "but Michael may know differently."

"I see. What does he do for a living?"

"He's some kind of scientist. He goes on lecture tours. It's all rather vague in my mind."

"Well," Dr. Alden said, looking at his watch, "the

mad mongrels seem to have retired to their lairs. I think I'll get out of here." He rose and clasped my elbows in his hands. "You sit tight for another twenty-four hours. Lock your doors and don't let anyone in. Give them both their medication and they ought to be showing considerable improvement by then. Now, I'm not going to rush off and stir up a fuss about all this until I can think of a way to get you three out of here, and that won't be possible for another week. But, in the meantime, I'm going to notify the Medical Association about Raphael's goings-on. They ought to keep him busy for a while answering questions. We don't want to let *him* get away in that trailer of his, do we? We want him behind bars, where he belongs. Do you think you can stick it out a little longer?"

"I think so," I said. "My main concern is getting food for my patients. I bribed one of the maids to set trays outside my door whenever possible, but they may discharge her now."

"You're a brave girl," he said. "Tighten your belt and prepare for a sit-in. Remember, I'm out there figuring out something to do. Why don't I telephone that friend of yours in the city and tell him about your predicament? He can camp out there somewhere close and keep an eye out for anything unusual. Would that make you feel any better?"

I ran to get my purse where I had put Charles's home and office numbers. It was gone! "Someone was in my rooms," I said, "one day when I was gone. That's what they must have been looking for."

"Hm-m, seems like it was. Well, never mind—they didn't count on my barging in here. *I* can find him easily enough in the city directory. I'll get him for you and tell him to keep out of sight and do a little sleuthing on his own."

"Doctor, how can I thank you? Do be careful on your way out. Jock is old, but he's stout and strong. He might be lying in wait for you."

"They're too smart for that, girl. Even if they managed to pop me one, there would be too many questions about my disappearance. They don't want that. The best thing is to let them think I came and went without seeing anything out of the ordinary."

"But the poisoning? You said something to Vivian about that."

"She's all set to lay that at your door, remember? No, I think if we both lie low for a week until our patients are better, we'll have a chance to round them all up for some very embarrassing questions. And don't you worry about being implicated, either. My word is acceptable in these parts."

We shook hands solemnly. I hated to see him go more than I would admit to him. I cautiously opened the door and found the corridor empty.

"Be careful of the man in the trailer," I whispered. "He's the worst of them all."

Dr. Alden was swallowed up in the darkness, the only person outside who knew of the danger that lurked in this house.

CHAPTER 11

The harassment of my patients and me began with the dawn.

The three Livingstons relayed each other in pounding on the door, shouting epithets and threats. Vivian pleaded with Mrs. Regent to make me unlock the door.

"Who will do your hair, madam? You know that I am the only one who can attend you properly. Please, Mrs. Regent, let your Vivian in to help you."

Mrs. Regent was either only half-conscious of the pleas and general ado or she was still too weak to acknowledge the fuss. Occasionally, I was able to get some of the diminishing supply of milk and juice into her, and the dimercaprol was beginning to have an alleviative effect on her system. Her hair, usually so elaborately coiffed, I brushed regularly. I was careful, too, to bathe her frequently. But the bed linen was now limp and wrinkled, and there was no way for me to get clean garments or linen.

"Don't fret about it," she told me meekly. "You are doing the best you can."

"You don't blame me, then, for sending for Dr. Alden?" I insisted, anxious for her confidence in me.

"Why would they want to do this to me?" she asked miserably. Her eyes were circled with dark patches. "Is it my fault?"

"No," I said fondly, "of course not. You were under unhealthy influences."

"But—faith? Isn't that a blessing?"

"Not faith in ourselves," I said. "Only faith in God. Of ourselves we are nothing. We must throw ourselves on God's mercy and have faith in *Him*."

"Who is in the other room, Marly?"

I knew that to tell her now would be too much of a shock in her weakened condition. I must wait until Michael's return. "It is a young girl I found on the dunes very ill," I temporized. "She has pneumonia."

"Then don't let me keep you from her."

She slept a great deal now that she was eased from the paroxysms of nausea and diarrhea. If only I could keep the Livingstons from bothering her.

One afternoon, when both she and Annette were asleep, I threw myself down on the loveseat and dozed off. The rain had cleared away, leaving an overcast sky with a strong wind blowing. Something awakened me, and I had a feeling that I was not alone. I ran to Mrs. Regent's room and there, on the balcony, I saw Vivian crouched. She looked so miserable, limned against the dark sky in her shabby sweater, that for a moment I was aware of a great pity for her. She had been Mrs. Regent's pet for most of her adult life. Surely remorse must have set in now that she realized the depth of her betrayal.

I made certain that the balcony doors were locked, then I spoke to her. "There is nothing you can do here, Vivian. Please go before you catch cold."

"Can't I just see her through the glass?" she begged hoarsely. "Pull back the curtains and let me see her."

"You want Mrs. Regent to get well, don't you, Vivian? Then go away and let her rest."

Mrs. Regent roused. "Let the poor thing in, Marly,"

she said. "She isn't to blame. Vivian's is a morose and antagonistic nature."

In response to her sweetness, I pulled back the curtains. "Wave at her, then, so that she'll see you are all right."

This accomplished, Vivian crept away. But the fact remained that they were going to starve us out, or worse. I felt sorry for Vivian, but I couldn't place any credence in her concern.

"She was only a child." Mrs. Regent began on one of her past reminiscences. "Utterly incompatible with her parents and, for that reason, gravitating toward me. I used to let her play with my jewel boxes for amusement. I promised her that one day, when she was older, I'd give her a gem or two for her very own. From then on, she delegated herself as my devoted servant, even going so far as to take a course in hairdressing so that my own beautician could be dismissed."

The tale was told in kindness, but something of its incongruity struck me. Had Vivian's life been warped by this careless promise? Had she seen a way of escape from her servile attachment by acquiring some of the jewels? Or had she coveted them all?

"Where are the jewels now?" I asked.

An almost crafty expression came into Mrs. Regent's eyes. "Not until I am gone," she said with a cunning that I had not seen before. "I have been forced to protect myself, you see."

"Then you have never trusted Vivian?"

"I have never completely trusted her parents," she amended. "And *she* was entirely under their domination." She went on slowly, saving her breath: "Mrs. Livingston is the brains—Jock, the brawn—and Vivian the tool."

"Then, why, knowing all this, did you put yourself in their hands?"

She smiled wearily. "Put yourself in my place, Marly. What would you have done? Would you not have provided some insurance for yourself in return for care and—service?"

So she had suspected for a long time, I thought pityingly as yet another question occurred to me. "Then why did you let the faith healer come?"

"That, too, was a compromise, I'm afraid. I had long dwelt in a spiritual desert, only concerned with myself and my own grief. Vivian seemed to bloom under his influence, and she spoke of nothing else until I agreed to see him. He seemed to be a holy and soothing person—almost hypnotic. He advocated self-reliance in a most persuasive way."

Yes, I thought, Clarence could do that. It would gratify him to take advantage of one old and weak, with or without the jewels for an inspiration. Essentially, the power over another, the satisfaction it gave him, would be enough for him.

Annette stirred, and I left Mrs. Regent to go to her.

"I'm hungry, Darling!"

"You're always hungry," I teased, glad to see her returning to normalcy. I gave her a sip of milk and two vitamins. "We have to conserve our food supply until someone comes to bring help," I explained.

"What's 'conserve'?"

"Save. Save the milk."

"Oh." She seemed satisfied with her own understanding. "Who is in there talking?"

"That is Mrs. Regent. She is sick, too."

"I want to see her."

"Not now," I said, imagining the shock to the woman at seeing the reincarnation of Sylvia before her. "Some other day, when she is well again."

"Am I well?"

"Not for a while, darling." I hugged her to me affectionately, happy that she was safe for the moment. Perhaps they were gathering their forces for another onslaught, but for the present we were safe. "You are beautiful," I told her. "And you are my own darling."

The days dragged interminably, hunger gnawing at us all in ever-increasing agony, the weather bleak and cheerless. Oh yes, they were counting now on my coming out for food. They had retired to wait while my patients gained strength and appetite, and I had three more days of depriving them before I could hope for release for them, and for me. Had Charles come? I could not see the dunes from any of these front windows, only the gates, which were closed and locked against any merciful invaders.

Once I glimpsed Jock taking the mail from the postman. What if I opened the windows and called to the man, asking him to send help and food? I felt a searing temptation to do so. But Dr. Alden had asked me to sit it out. *He* was the only one I could depend on, and I must do as he had asked. I spent long hours at the windows, fighting hunger pangs as I gazed out over the expanse that meant freedom and dreaming of dramatic rescue by shining knights bearing thick hamburgers. My mouth would water and my eyes blur with loneliness and dejection. If Charles knew, he would come. Had Dr. Alden been unable to reach him after all?

Michael, too, began to take on the attributes of a knight in my fogged mind. I could imagine him— kind, concerned, reliable, and strong—throwing the Livingstons out into the fog and providing for us all with that special dependability which his lazy attitude cloaked.

Another day I saw Delphia going to the gates with

a bag in each hand. She walked with brisk determination in spite of her bulk, and I wondered, fascinated, how she would manage to get through the gates. She was rattling them uselessly when Jock appeared and motioned her back. Delphia appeared to be giving him an argument when he gestured threateningly. After a moment, she turned and walked back to the house. So she was a prisoner, too?

"No one enters and no one leaves," the bartender had said. I remembered with chagrin that Charles and I had laughed at the "legend" of Regent Manor. Oh, the cleverness of those who had inculcated the belief in the village that the old castle was filled with haunts and odd characters who resented any invasion of privacy!

That night, I was aroused from a fitful sleep by footsteps in the corridor—heavy steps, half-running. There followed a rapid knocking on my door.

"Marly, let me in—quickly!"

It was Charles!

I threw open the door and clung to him, shaking, heedless of the bundles he carried.

"There now—take it easy, old girl. The cook let me in the back way and gave me some food for you."

Glad as I was to see him, the food meant even more. I reminded myself of Annette as I tore off a piece of bread and stuffed it into my mouth.

"Oh, Charles, where have you been?" I said between mouthfuls.

"Getting married," he said smugly. "BJ and I went to Reno last week. That's why I wasn't there when your call was relayed by some doctor-chap."

There was tea, hot and strong and bitter, cookies and cake—somewhat stale, but delicious for all that —a cold pork chop, two chicken legs, and several thin slices of roast beef.

"It's all there was," Charles said somewhat defensively. "My Lord, Marly, what have you let yourself in for? The cook was incoherent—murder, poisoning, the works. Do you suppose that food is safe to eat?"

"Oh, Charles, you're married!" I said, tears of relief and gratitude flowing down my face. "I thought *I* was the light of your life. BJ got you, did she?"

"Never mind all that. I had the very devil of a time getting to you—for days I've been out there trying to get a glimpse of you, and freezing half to death myself. Then today I saw the fat woman—turned out to be the cook—mixing it up with the caretaker. I slipped around to the kitchen door under cover of darkness and managed to get her attention. She almost yanked me inside, so glad was she to find a deliverer."

"How did you get into the grounds?"

"You told me once about a cyclone fence, remember?"

"Oh, Charles, it's been horrible!"

"There, there, don't steam up, now it's nearly over. The doctor's had a nasty job on his hands, but he has his evidence now. The trailer chap talked."

"Clarence?"

"You know the blighter?"

I couldn't wait another minute to awaken my patients and share the nourishment with them. Annette's wide eyes regarded Charles as though he were the Archangel Michael while he poured tea into a mug and gave it to her sparingly. For Mrs. Regent, I fixed a dainty repast, using the best cup and sectioning an orange.

"So it was your Mr. Christian who came to our aid," she said. "I suppose now you'll be marrying him in gratitude, if for no other reason."

Laughter bubbled to my lips in near-hysteria, startling us both for a moment. "BJ got him, after all," I said in mock-humility. "Oh, Mrs. Regent, we're almost out of this now! God does hear prayer."

"And the girl? Is she all right?"

"Her name is Annette," I said gently. I watched her face to see if the name meant anything to her, but she retained her sprightly look of interest. "You're going to become very fond of her, I know, in days to come."

She laid her hand on mine. "It's you I'm fond of, my dear. What would either of us have done without you?" She looked dangerously near to hysteria. When she had regained her composure, she said, "Where is that splendid young man? I wish to congratulate him."

Somewhere outside an owl screeched. I wondered if Michael would think I had fulfilled his trust.

CHAPTER 12

Annette was curled at her grandmother's feet before the fire.

Michael leaned nonchalantly against the mantel, as perfectly relaxed as though the whole world had not come tumbling down around our heads a few hours ago. He was watching the young girl and Mrs. Regent with that glint of affection in his eyes that had given me my first inclination of confidence in his motives, no matter how suspect they had seemed at the time.

I cleared the tea-things away, noting with gratitude and some amusement that every crumb had been devoured. "Nothing more," I said when Annette would have begged for another biscuit. "We're having a bountiful feast at dinnertime, just the four of us."

Michael touched my hand as I passed by. "I think it's time for the whole story now," he said under his breath, "and I want you here."

I looked into his face anxiously, and saw the wisdom and security there. "Whatever you say, Michael, of course. Still, there has been quite a lot of excitement, with the police here and—"

"Neither of your patients was aware of that," he said reassuringly. He regarded them fondly. "With their stomachs filled for the time being, I think the time has come for revelation."

I went to the kitchen and checked the roasting meat while I washed the tea-things. The aroma of cooking food, the warmth of the cheery room, gave me a feeling of inspiration. Delphia, the only innocent one in this den of iniquity, was in her room, sleeping after her long vigil. The climate was right for Michael's story, and he appeared eager to get it told. I washed my hands and went back to the group before the fire.

Mrs. Regent had recovered remarkably. Her eyes were as bright as ever, and although her lovely white hair hung over her shoulders in braids, she was once again alert, and curious about all that had transpired during her interval of unawareness. From time to time, her eyes rested on Annette's bright head at her knee, and she touched the smooth tresses. Was it possible, I wondered, that she sensed the child's identity?

Annette, still very thin and pale, seemed content to watch "the little men dancing in the fire," and I hoped that she would not understand all that Michael was about to tell us. By the same token, I hoped that *I* would.

He had come over the front gates, as agile as an alley cat, by the simple expedient of climbing on top of his car and dropping down. It seemed an eternity ago that Charles and I had watched him from our prison upstairs, then heard his voice on the telephone asking for the police. Mrs. Livingston had expostulated, her voice smooth and convincing at first, then rising to near-hysteria. We had heard a scuffle of feet and Jock's curses before Michael was at our door, his eyes taking in the situation at once.

"Stay with them," he told Charles without greeting, "until I clear these parasites out of the house."

There had been an interval of sirens screaming up the road, of Vivian's shrieking denials in response to the calm, authoritative questions of the policemen, then silence.

Charles had been the first to recover his equilibrium when all the fuss was over. "If you'll excuse me," he said with an exaggerated bow, "I have a fairly recent bride awaiting my return in San Francisco."

I saw Michael's eyes flick from Charles to me in surprise. "I don't think I understand."

"Never mind that now," I said. I kissed Charles on the cheek. "Thanks for coming, my friend. When I've had time to sort this all out in my mind, I'm sure I'll be more than ever grateful. Give BJ my love, will you, and best wishes for you both?"

The next hours were busy ones. Michael went to the village and returned with supplies; then he built a roaring fire in the library and helped me take the patients down from the scene of their captivity. When they were settled, I brought a light tea to assuage the hunger that had become a state of being for all of us.

Now I looked at Michael, waiting for him to begin. I had a million questions, but they could wait until he had had his say. Mrs. Regent broke the silence.

"There was no money, was there, Michael?"

His eyes met hers, and he shook his head. "Not for a long time, Aunt Marian—but that is not the issue just now."

"I still have my jewels," she said anxiously.

Michael waved a hand to dismiss the subject. "There is something much more important." He nodded toward Annette. "It concerns something I have done that I thought was for the best."

I saw Mrs. Regent give a start. Instinctively, she reached out to clasp Annette's hand in her own. It was as though she knew, yet was waiting for Michael to corroborate her knowledge.

He began slowly, filling his pipe with hands that

were a trifle unsteady. "I asked Marly to be here," he said with a wry smile, "because only Heaven knows what she has thought of me. But I am free now to divulge the secret that I have held, alone, for almost fourteen years."

He went into the circumstances of Sylvia's last illness with all the tact and delicacy he could summon. She had learned shortly after her husband's death that she was pregnant with his child. Detained in England for many months during the settling of his estate, she had become obsessed with the idea that her grief would afflict the child, either mentally or physically, and had called Michael's father, Dr. Davidson, who had ordered her back to the States at once.

"She put him off," Michael said, "For one reason or another. When Sylvia finally agreed to come, she insisted on coming by ship. Dad made all the reservations for her, agreeing that the interval of rest might settle her imaginings. He was totally unprepared, you see, for all that was to follow."

Mrs. Regent had straightened in her chair, and the blue of her eyes, which had deepened with emotion, never left Michael's face.

"Sylvia died in childbirth, then?"

He nodded, pity clouding his face. "Yes, Aunt Marian, she died giving birth to Annette."

I saw the woman strain toward the child with maternal hunger. But she refrained from gathering her close, sensing, perhaps, that Annette must be spared the trauma of this sad recital.

"Everything was done for her—everything. You must believe that."

"Go on, Michael."

"When my father and the others were unable to save Sylvia, they turned their attention to the baby.

The birth had been difficult, and there was a dislocation of Annette's spine. My father had promised Sylvia that you must not know of the birth if the child were abnormal in any way. She had made over all of hers and Clive's money to him for the child's care."

Mrs. Regent tore her eyes away from Michael to stare at the perfection of Annette, who lay full length before the fire. The girl was so lovely that it took one's breath.

Michael put another log on the fire and stirred it to flame. Delphia, freshened by her nap, passed the doorway with an indifferent glance at us. She would go down to the kitchen, I knew, and occupy herself in preparing a festive dinner. The fire crackled with new life and Michael resumed his seat.

"When my father died," he said simply, "he passed his solemn promise on to me: you were not to know of the child's existence until, or if, she became entirely well. Otherwise, she would be cared for by the money from her parents' estate for life."

"How pitiful!" Mrs. Regent exclaimed involuntarily. "That poor, tiny child—without love!"

"It was a hard bargain for me to keep," Michael assented, "during the years that followed. One operation succeeded another, each an improvement in the spinal condition, until it was possible to move Annette to a therapy institution where, for the first time in her life, she was taught to walk."

"How old was she then?" My own voice sounded strained and raw to my ears.

"Nearly six. I went to see her regularly, and she came to know me. But there was evidence of retardation, and she was completely dependent on those who cared for her."

"But she is *not* retarded," I protested.

Michael regarded me with interest, and something

like respect. "You are probably the first person to discover that. But without schooling, except in the physical aspects of her case, she was like a child of three —gurgling more than speaking. By now, she was seven years old and the therapy institution was forced to close because of lack of funds." He turned to Mrs. Regent. "I was faced, too, with the necessity of providing for you, Aunt Marian. Sylvia had expressly specified that you must spend the rest of your days in this place that meant so much to you. I only mention this, dear, so that you'll see the reason for my more stringent economies."

"I should have known," Mrs. Regent murmured penitently. "It must have cost a very great deal."

"A very great deal," Michael repeated. "But worth every penny. However, you can understand that Sylvia's and Clive's money was running out because of mountainous hospital expenses. That was when I began selling off parcels of Manor property—robbing Peter to pay Paul, as it were."

"And I thought that I was rich and you were— stingy. I *am* sorry, Michael!"

"You *are* rich," Michael said fondly, glancing at Annette, "in other things than money. But let me go on. At this point, I was forced to make a decision for the good of all concerned, so I adopted the only alternative I could think of—to bring Annette to Regent Manor." He gestured with the hand that held the pipe. "Oh, I know now, looking back, that I could have arranged the whole thing much better. But at the time I was harassed by the need to further my own career in order to obtain money. I was, as yet, completely unknown, of course. So I—mistakenly, I know now—took Livvie into my confidences and put Annette into her care before I left for France and England on my first lecture tour. Fortunately, it was a success and I was offered a teaching chair in science in a French university. That enabled me to send money home to Mrs. Livingston for Annette's care and for the upkeep of the premises here."

There were tears in Mrs. Regent's eyes. "Michael, Michael, what have we done to you?"

He made a gesture of self-disparagement. "I was only carrying out a solemn vow to my father," he reminded her. "I was doing what I wanted to do, however badly." He paused a moment before he continued sadly: "Imagine my consternation when I returned after four years to discover that no provisions had been made for Annette's mental progress. She was almost twelve years old, and still a child. Her vocabulary was limited to that of a kindergartner, and she ran the beaches and forests like a wild animal—"

"And I never knew," Mrs. Regent said on a sob.

"I took Mrs. Livingston to task," Michael continued, "and she seemed to respect me for it, although she was obdurate in protesting her own helplessness in the matter. Annette, she told me, was incorrigible. She was uncivilized and should not, under any circumstances, be presented to you as your grandchild. She refused to live in the house, she survived on wild berries and scraps, and her manners were atrocious. All this was more or less true at the time."

"But she responds to love and attention," I interjected. "You should have tried to get acquainted with her."

"Don't blame him, my dear," Mrs. Regent said weakly. "He was only a boy, and he has had so much responsibility." She sighed, and I could see that she was very tired. I placed a stool under her feet and drew the coverlet over them. She ignored my gesture, willing Michael to go on with his tale.

"I tried that—within limitations," Michael said. "All that summer I pored over the most basic instruction books with her. She hated me for curtailing her freedom. I insisted that she eat and sleep in the house, only to find that she slipped out in the night to her own world." He ran his fingers through his hair in distracted remembrance. "In the fall, when I was to set off on another lecture series, I was convinced that Livvie was right, that Annette was hopeless in a social analysis and should be allowed to pursue her happiness in her own way. I felt, along with the housekeeper, that to introduce her to her grandmother would impose an impossible burden on a sick woman. I didn't know then, as I do now, that the Livingstons saw Annette as a threat to whatever they hoped Vivian was to obtain from you, Aunt Marian."

"A careless remark about my jewels." Mrs. Regent sighed, "And their greed exceeded all decency. Naturally, they would resent Annette and any claim she might have on my affections. Michael, why didn't you tell me?"

"Mainly because I'd had Mrs. Livingston's promise to spend more time with the girl, give her more love and training. I hoped, you see, that Annette would tame down as she grew older and that she would respond to the basic fundamentals of behavior." He leaned forward intensely. "You wouldn't believe, seeing her as she is now, how wild and unruly she was. She had tantrums like a little cat, clawing and shrieking and kicking shins." He permitted himself a wry smile. "I was her victim more than once."

Annette stirred and looked up at me pleadingly. "Darling, I'm hungry."

"Why does she call you that?" Michael asked.

"Perception," I retorted, "of a kind we 'more civilized' persons don't have. She has learned to trust me."

"Ah!" Michael said ruefully. "You have imposed no restrictions on her—is that it?"

"Partly," I admitted. "You see, I didn't know who she was, or where she came from. And the occasion of our first meeting was during a thunderstorm that frightened her. She slept in my room that night and —well, it seemed to establish a rapport between us from then on."

"I remember now," Mrs. Regent said gently, "that I heard voices once or twice. I wondered at the time. It may interest you to know that Vivian and her mother objected violently to your having the suite adjoining mine."

"A part of the ensuing plot," Michael ventured. "You see, the money was running out and they meant to kill you before the jewels, too, were gone."

Mrs. Regent's hand brushed her forehead. "It seems incomprehensible, sitting here with all of you. But it's true! I had done a great deal of promising, you see, to assure their loyalty and devotion in my helplessness. But they liked you, Michael, and they must have assumed that you would be the heir to my nonexistent fortune. Why didn't they plan to do away with you, too?"

"They probably had that in mind," Michael said, unperturbed, "for the future. But Marly's unexpected appearance must have thrown the original plan into confusion. She, too, would have to be done away with, don't you see? It became a vicious circle, one murder following another, until they were obliged to enlist the aid of the faith healer." He turned to me. "By the way, did I understand you to say that you know this man?" I nodded, and he said, "That alone would have been enough to incriminate you if I had known. I wasn't entirely sure of you, in any case."

"Then why did you hire me?"

His eyes strayed to his aunt. "I think you must have begun to suspect something, didn't you?"

She stirred restlessly. "Vivian had become more and more unmanageable. She scolded all the time, and it was apparent that some force was being exerted on her."

"Clarence Gibbs," I said. "Your Dr. Raphael. According to Delphia, she was in love with him."

"Delphia must have some revealing secrets to divulge," Michael said quietly. "But how did *you* happen to suspect foul play?"

I tried to think. How had it all begun? I shook my head in perplexity. "So many things kept popping up —some of them having to do with Annette, but not all. Let's not go into all that right now. What I want to know, Michael, is when *you* became suspicious."

"I came down here to camp not so long ago," Michael said. "Two of my fellow scientists from New York wished to study the flora and fauna adjoining California beaches, and on an impulse I offered to bring them down here. We pitched camp in a sheltered cove near the beach and—" He interrupted himself to regard his aunt questioningly. "I assumed it would be all right, even though I myself am largely responsible for posting the No Trespassing signs to keep out the curious. I played right into the hands of the Livingstons on that one."

"I've often wondered about that," Mrs. Regent ruminated. "I thought it was being done for my sake, but I was never able to divine the reason behind so much passion for privacy."

"Mostly it was because of Annette," Michael said softly.

Annette, hearing her name, roused from her scrutiny of the flames. "I want to eat," she said willfully. "I'm hungry."

I laughed and rose. "This is par for the course," I told the others. "I'll go tell Delphia that we're ready."

On the way to the kitchen regions, my heart felt light with the divulging of Michael's long-secret burden. I had so wanted him to be blameless, in spite of all my suspicions, and now that I was convinced he had done his best for the sakes of all concerned, I felt a warm surge of respect and admiration for him. He had made mistakes, but they were honest mistakes, and his frankness in admitting them was reassuring. He was really a splendid person, sacrificing himself and his own means to carry out Sylvia's and his father's deathbed wishes.

I felt almost happy again as I asked Delphia to serve dinner and sit with us. Little did I guess that the long trauma was not yet ended, nor that the worst was yet to come.

CHAPTER 13

There was little opportunity during those next weeks to do much about Annette's mental development. I was kept busy trying to fill Vivian's place in caring for Mrs. Regent, doing her hair and taking charge of the myriad details that Vivian, for all her moroseness, had carried on so admirably. Then, too, there were the duties of Rose and Kate to assume—all that cleaning and laundering, endless lists for Michael to take to market, visits from Dr. Alden to prepare for and sit in on, even though Mrs. Regent was gaining strength and was almost well again.

The little man who had braved the dangers of Regent Manor in those dark days to bring his skill and medicines to the two desperately sick patients had become dear to all of us. He was conscientious and kind, although outwardly stern of manner, and his interest in all of us was apparent. I had long since told him of Michael's innocence in the matter, and now the two were on congenial terms.

On a certain balmy evening, I found them on the terrace enjoying their highballs and cigars. The sinking sun shone like rubies on the tops of cypress and fir. From somewhere out over the ocean a gull gave his startled cry, and it echoed through the air. Annette's sweet laugh came from her grandmother's room and Mrs. Regent's voice droned on in one of her interminable recollections of the child's parents, Sylvia and Clive. I sank into a chair as Michael half-rose.

Dr. Alden smiled at me. "Now that the criminals have been tried and the date of their sentences set, we're planning an escape for you."

"Escape?" I repeated wonderingly. "You mean, I'm not needed here anymore?"

"You need a vacation," Michael said. "A change of scene. How would you like to take Annette to San Francisco for a week or so? Dr. Alden has found a capable woman to look after my aunt and I've hired Kate and Rose back. They were not implicated in the crime, you know, and they get along very well with Delphia."

I hesitated, accepting the brandy that Michael brought to me, and swirling it around in the snifter absently. I was very tired, but content, too. I glanced up at Michael worriedly. "I don't think that I ever want to leave here—even for a week."

He sat down on the broad arm of my wicker chair and said persuasively, "It's not only my concern for *you*, Marly, although Lord knows you've been through enough, even without the strictly manual labor of these past months." His hand touched mine. "Aside from all that, it's Annette I'm thinking of. You've said that you'd like to take her to her first movie—her first concert—and I know it would mean a great deal to her to experience these things with you as guide." He resumed his own chair and began the familiar ritual of filling his pipe with tobacco. "I want you to take her on a shopping spree, too. Buy her all the nice things a girl her age should have."

Dr. Alden laughed. "That ought to intrigue any woman."

"But—but I can't just leave like that," I protested. "Mrs. Regent might not like it."

"She's all for it," Michael assured me.

"Then—what about the Livingstons and Clarence Gibbs? I'd feel much easier if they were off serving their respective sentences. Aren't they out on bail?"

Dr. Alden and Michael exchanged glances before the doctor said, "This is one reason we want you and the girl out of the way for a while. Most of their animosity seemed to be directed at you and her during the trial. Mrs. Regent will be quite safe with Michael and the servants about, but Annette—" He turned his palms upward. "Who can say when she'll take a notion to roam about the grounds? One of them, or some associate of theirs, might harm her."

"Why are they out of jail?" I raged. "They tried to kill Mrs. Regent and undoubtedly would have disposed of Annette, too, in time. Why aren't they under lock and key—all of them?"

"The law, Miss Carewe, is fair and just, and bail is legal. In another week, they'll begin serving their sentences."

"All right," I said wearily, "I'll go for Annette's sake —and to keep her out of harm's way."

Michael drew a sigh of relief. "You can see your friends, the Christians," he said a bit too cheerfully, "and my aunt is delighted to have Annette exposed to culture. I'll make reservations for you at the Fairmont, and you two will have a great time."

"Yes," I said dubiously, "it will be very nice, I'm sure."

"Then it's settled," Dr. Alden said, rising. "If it's any consolation to you, I'll breathe easier, too, when the four of them are off to prison. You'll drive the girls in tomorrow, Michael?"

"Oh no!" I said quickly. "I couldn't take Michael away from here." I raised my brows at Michael. "Couldn't I take the Manor car and drive us myself?"

"Take mine," he said. He walked the doctor to the driveway, and I sat on dreaming of the places we would go, of all the things I would show Annette. The sky darkened to deep purple and on its velvet sheen first one star, then another appeared. Annette had never been to a zoo, or a department store, or a museum, or to church. She had never had a ribbon for her hair, or rings and bracelets. I thought of the childish delight the simplest pleasures would give her, and I felt my enthusiasm for the little trip grow to magnificent proportions. I must be careful not to spoil her with too much indulgence all at once. I heard the doctor's car leave, and soon Michael returned, his pipe glowing in the dusk.

"This is the first time in many years that I've felt free," he said, seating himself on the balustrade. He looked up at the lighted windows above us. "To have the secret off my mind is like a great weight removed. And to know that I can make adequate financial arrangements for their futures has given me a new lease on life."

"There *is* money, then?"

"Yes. I've been able to lease a part of the beach for oceanography experiments—a good long lease that will more than take care of current expenses and insure Annette's education. Her grandmother has an obsession that the child will one day be a musician, that *her* fingers will take the place of my aunt's. This afternoon, I found them in the music room going over the scales, and Annette was much interested and quite apt, I might say."

"It must be a relief to you," I agreed fondly, "to

have them together. Do you think Annette fully understands?"

"Aunt Marian will see to that with her usual tact. She reserves that particular privilege for herself and —have you noticed?—it has done her a lot of good. Dr. Alden said as much."

A silence fell, and I saw a star describe a brief little dance before it fell into oblivion in a blazing trail. Matt and I had wished upon a falling star on soft summer evenings such as this in Kansas. What would I wish? To stay here forever. To have Michael near, his pipe in his mouth, and the four of us making a life of happiness in this old house that had witnessed so much of misery, of grief and sorrow. His strong profile was etched against the lights of the open French doors, and I felt a catch of my breath. Had there ever been a time when I did not know this man, or when we had been enemies? I could not believe it, so close was he to me now.

"What will you do," I asked, low, "when this is all settled?"

His head turned in surprise. "Didn't I just tell you? I'll take part in the ocean experiments."

"Right here?" I felt a surge of joy. He would not be leaving, after all! He would not be going away on those mysterious tours, or teaching in some faraway university. My eyes lifted to the place where the star had fallen. Had I actually wished for this?

"Michael, what brought you home when we needed you so?"

He paced the length of the veranda before he slumped down in a chair and said incredibly, "You!" There was a long pause before he said again, "Yes, you, Marly."

"I don't think I understand."

His laugh was shaky. "Nor do I. Call it internal combustion, or something. No sooner had I gone away than I found myself thinking about you day and night—the way you were with them all, your poise and humor and laugh, and the way you walk—everything about you. I knew you didn't trust me, and it began to bother me. For some reason, I wanted to establish myself in your opinion and estimation—wanted to tell you the truth, the whole truth." He reached out for my hand and held it. "I was jealous, too. I could picture Christian hanging about and making points with you in my absence." He laughed shortly at his own absurdity and asked, "By the way, what ever happened to that budding romance? He was crazy about you, I know. Even Aunt Marian saw it. But—you? Neither of us could figure out your feelings in the matter."

"Never mind that," I said lightly. Something told me that this was the beginning of a revelation for which I had secretly hoped, but which frightened me, nevertheless. "So that's what brought you home early from the lecture tour?"

"The lecture tour, yes." He gave a bitter "Ha!" and repeated, "The lecture tour." His fingers tightened on mine. "Darling, would you lose all respect for me if I told you that I didn't know enough? I had taken Von Hagen's place on several occasions and managed to bumble through fairly well. This other chap, however, was a different matter. I realized that I was incapable of a serious career in my chosen field until I had studied more about it. That's when I began to explore the possibilities of leasing some of this land for experimentation. It was a perfect setup, and I was able to stimulate enough interest in the project to put it under consideration." He stood before me, every line of his body intent and strained. "I could ask you to marry me now, Marly." Very gently, he lifted me from my chair, and our eyes clung for a moment. "I love you," he said very softly. "I want you to be my wife."

It was all so sudden, and I wanted to say that, until I thought how trite it would sound to him. And yet, wasn't it what had been in the back of my mind ever since Mrs. Regent had begun her matchmaking? When Michael was gone and I had longed for him, I had supposed that it was his strength I wanted in my fear. Now I knew that it was something more as his head came closer to mine and our lips met in a shattering kiss. Michael loved me! He had spent his life for others and now he was free to claim his own happiness. I clung to him, hardly able to speak.

"Well, darling?" he asked anxiously. "Have I been too premature?"

"I never dreamed—" I began. "I thought of you so much, too, Michael, but—"

"You sweet girl!" He clasped me to him with an ardor that threatened every bone in my body. "You're sure?"

The thin moon drifted higher and there followed an interval of lovers' remembering. When did I first know? he asked. And what did I think when he returned so unceremoniously? Was I sure that I wanted to spent the rest of my life in this mossy old mansion where I had experienced so much fear and horror? The questions continued while I was in Michael's arms, and the answers must have been satisfactory, for he was almost boyish in his exuberance as he made plans for our future.

Everything I had ever wanted had been suddenly made mine, I thought as I made ready for bed later in my moonlit room. I had found a fine man to love me, a home, and the two people whom I loved almost as dearly as Michael were to be my family. I drifted off to sleep on a blissful cloud.

The low, sobbing moan of distant foghorns intruded on the murky morning, bringing me to reluctant awareness as I opened my eyes to the cascade of closed golden velvet draperies at the window of my bedroom in the Fairmont Hotel. I groaned with felicity and burrowed back into the pillows to let my drowsy mind bask in the luxurious somnolence of half-sleep, half-wakefulness, before I jerked to with a start. Annette and I had a busy day before us—prowling the hidden shops and quaint side streets of San Francisco before going to Playland-at-the-Beach. I looked at her lying in the companion bed so peacefully asleep, and thanked God that she was safely here with me, far away from the grim threat of Regent Manor and whatever diabolical designs Clarence Gibbs might be plotting against her.

After a luxurious stretch and a call to Room Service for our breakfast, I walked to the shrouded windows and pulled the draperies wide to expose the misty view below—the regal haughtiness of the Pacific Union Club, the towers of Grace Cathedral beyond, and farther still, shrouded in fog, the beach where I would take Annette later in the day for a fun visit to Playland.

I showered in haste, hoping the sun would burn away the morning fog, and opened the door from the bathroom to find Annette already dressed in warm clothes and sturdy shoes, her face glowing with expectancy. How like any young fourteen-year-old girl she looked now, and I felt a vague pang for the return of the little waif who had leaned on me so expectantly a few months ago. So much had changed, so many lives had taken unforeseen paths since my introduction to Regent Manor that rainy night.

Annette caught my hands in her slim, cold ones. "We *are* going to the beach, aren't we, Darling? I'm wearing my sweater—and I ate all my breakfast—"

I laughingly pulled her close for a hug just as the telephone rang. It was Michael, sounding so close that I wondered if he had decided to follow us, after all. But he said quickly, "Are you doing all right? I wanted to call earlier, but Aunt Marian was afraid I'd awaken you. How's Annette? Enjoying herself?"

"We both are," I assured him. "We've bought enough clothes to last her for a lifetime, and she's as vain as a peacock. It's been heavenly, Michael—but I do miss you! It would be perfect if you were here."

There was a short pause before he said huskily, "I love you, Sweetheart. Do you realize how very much?" I closed my eyes, my heart soaring with joy before he asked abruptly, "What are your plans for today? I want to be able to picture you and be less lonely."

I told him that we were going to Playland for lunch and to spend the day doing all the things that Annette wanted. It was only later, when we had hung up, that it occurred to me that Michael and Dr. Alden were more concerned for our young protegee's safety than they let on. But why? What would be the point of Clarence trying to harm her now when Mrs. Regent knew of their kinship to each other? Obviously, there would be no monetary reward, as there might have been before. Besides, Clarence Gibbs knew that he was going to prison, and he surely wouldn't need money there.

I finished dressing, tossing the myriad possibilities for their solicitude about in my mind. Why were they so fearful? Kidnapping? Perhaps. For Mrs. Regent, and Michael, too, would give every cent that they could raise to ransom this precious girl—Mrs. Regent because she had found her beloved granddaughter and Michael because he still felt a deep sense of guilt that he had kept Annette's identity a secret, entrusting her care to the untrustworthy Livingstons. But we were far away from Clarence and danger, and whether he were sane or completely deranged, he could not possibly know where we were.

The sun did not pentrate the clouds today, and I took the precaution of taking a taxi to the beach, much to Annette's disappointment. An hour later, however, she was bouncing along beside me, awed and intrigued, as we strolled through the tawdry attractions of Playland. Bunting flapped soggily in the cold wind and lights were multi-colored blobs in the murky haze. The tinkling tune from the merry-go-round, the jeering laugh of the Fat Lady in the shrine over the Fun House, jarred my nerves. There was the phony atmosphere of a carnival that was not a carnival at all but was, instead, to my tormented imagination, a trap for the unaware tourists who crowded the sand-strewn streets and clogged into groups around the concessions.

"Mommy, I want to ride the roller coaster!"

The young woman in slacks, her hair in huge curlers under a sleazy pink scarf, jerked the small, whining boy along. "Carter, if you don't stop bawling, I'm going to take you right home, hear?"

Their voices dwindled off in the noises of the crowd, and the rancid smells of frying hamburgers and popcorn smote my nostrils. Annette, hungry as usual, tugged at my arm and gestured toward the hot-dog booth. I forced a smile. I must not let this peculiar mood of mine spoil her day. She munched contentedly as we made our way to the Fun House with its maze of distorted mirrors, blow machines, and screaming people. To me, there was an ominous aloneness in the teeming place, and I screamed involuntarily as the icy hand of a wooden skeleton dropped upon my shoulder. Annette laughed with glee at my fright and protested when I put my arm through hers to hold her near to me. A man whose features were elongated to hideous proportions in the full-length mirror ducked into the narrow passageway as we approached. He reminded me of Clarence, and I shivered. But I knew I was being foolish. His glasses were black, and Clarence's were thick and transparent. Nerves, that was all.

It was getting late when we came out of the Fun House, and I tried to persuade Annette to call it a day. We would ride back to the city, I promised persuasively, on the funny old rolling streetcar; then she could choose from among her pretty dresses and we would go to dinner.

"No! I don't want to," she cried with that stubborn defiance in her face that prefaced a tantrum. "I want popcorn!"

"All right, then," I said firmly, although I was secretly amused. "Popcorn—and then the streetcar." I saw it lumbering down the slope and hurried to a stand to buy the twin sacks. Several teen-aged boys with long hair and beads were haggling with the proprietor, and I was obliged to wait my turn. When I had paid, I turned to find Annette gone. Panic swelled in me until, my eyes sweeping over the crowd, I saw her climbing on the roller coaster.

I rushed to her, intending to give her a scolding, only to hear her announce gleefully, "A man gave me the ticket, Darling! Hurry! Hurry and come with me."

There was nothing to do but buy a ticket and pile on with her. I clutched the bar as the operator fastened it, and regretted my decision immediately as we began to roll. The train gained momentum as we reached the ascent, and I felt a new terror as I looked below at the peeling and flimsy pilings. There was hardly anyone else aboard—a man in a cap was hunched into his coat two seats ahead, and I wondered briefly why anyone would take this precipitous ride alone. For pleasure? I heard Annette's tinkling laughter as we neared the top. In another moment, we would go plummeting downward in a terrible rush of wind and shrieking steel rails, and I could feel the momentary pause of the car for the descent as I felt the nose drop and looked straight down into the abyss of the darkening day. My fingers tightened on the safety bar and I had motioned for Annette to do the same when, ahead of us, the man in the cap turned and *I looked into Clarence Gibbs's evil, twisted face!*

I screamed once before we toppled down with the force of a falling elevator. Up, down, up, down—the whole world was a blur of sky and lights and the sounds of Annette's screams of joy as we snapped around sharp curves, then spiraled downward, only to soar upward again in a rush that snapped my head back against the seat with a sharp bump.

Clarence! He was on this demon contrivance with us. He had followed us to the city, to Playland, and somehow—oh, dear Heaven! somehow he meant to kill us both. As we began another swift ascent, I screamed for the operator to stop the coaster, but my voice was whipped away on the wind and the blaring music. I saw a few bystanders laugh and point, pleased at my fright, and then they were gone and we were once more soaring around the curves, while the clammy wind slapped at my face and hair as we twisted and spiraled far above the receding earth, then plunged over the drops with such violence that I wondered what kept us from flying out of the car headfirst.

Suddenly, the wild motion seemed to slacken and gradually drop off, and the train creaked protestingly as it labored up the final height, the most terrifying summit of the gleaming rails, for a last assault into the abyss below. I drew a long breath and grasped Annette's arm in preparation for the worst of all. Then it stopped—just short of the top by a few feet!

In that instant, Clarence leaped to the car nearest us, his glasses gleaming opaquely above the threatening smile spread across his mouth. He scrambled into our seat, and I heard Annette's scream of recognition ring out before his hand closed around her throat. I moved to grapple with him and felt a fist smash into the side of my head. I reeled, stunned, and snapped back to reality in time to see him twist his hands into the hair of the terrified girl. He was forcing her body over the side, his own heavy body impervious to the blows I rained on his back and neck. Annette clung stubbornly to the bar, her fingers white at the knuckles.

"Clarence," I screamed. "It's Marly! Take me and let her go."

There was no recognition in the distorted face, and he mumbled something about watching us both fall, then gave a triumphant laugh that told me an accomplice waited at the controls below. Waited until he saw two bodies plummeting down and down before he would put the machine in motion again. As the three of us grappled in breathless violence against the death that loomed, I knew something else, too—that Clarence would go over the side with us. That was his crazed intention, out of his mind with hate and revenge. That would be his way out of the imprisonment, the defeat. In a last effort, I crashed my fists against his ears and felt his blow glance off my head before, scrambling for balance, his thick body lunged over the side with a long, croaking wail that sent spikes crawling along my nerves. Everything spun into lights and dizziness, fused into color and sound, before my eyes could focus on the figure crawling painstakingly up the crisscross network of wooden pilings—*Michael!*

The police brought our car down very slowly, I remember, while Michael held us both, sobbing, in his arms, and the sea of upturned faces became distinguishable. I remember the police cars and an ambulance, its red toplight flashing in dizzying arcs, and then my head was weightless and I slumped from Michael's arms in a dead faint.

CHAPTER 14

The El Camino Real was choked with cars. They crawled slowly along, almost bumper to bumper, and I dozed against Michael's shoulder, still groggy from the sedatives the doctor had given me to avert hysteria.

In the back seat, Annette chattered in excitement, but without any sign of distress from the macabre experience of the afternoon. Michael's tones were low and reassuring as he commented from time to time.

"I'm glad we're going home," Annette said at last, "to Grandmother." Her voice drifted off on a yawn. "I think I'll go to sleep now, Michael. Will you watch over Marly?"

"For the rest of my life," I heard him say fervently.

I stirred and touched his cheek with my fingers. He caught my hand and pressed it to his lips. "Michael, how did you know?" I asked sleepily. "Was it a premonition, or what?"

His strong face was still pale in the light from the dash, and I saw a line ripple along his jaw before he said, "While Gibbs was still in custody, a psychiatrists' team pronounced him paranoiac-schizophrenic —something of a persecution complex, as I understand it. Dr. Alden protested his release on bail on the strength of this, but his lawyer raised objections and he was let out. That of course was why Dr. Alden and I arranged for you to take Annette away. But after I called you, I began to think of the danger of Clarence Gibbs getting to you in a place like Playland—"

I sat up, fully awake now. "And how do you suppose Clarence knew where we were?"

Michael shook his head. "We'll never know the facts now," he said. "He might have been lurking about somewhere and seen the flurry of your departure. Or he may have been hiding and overheard our conversation on the terrace that night. In any case, he followed you. The morning I called you, I had taken a walk up to the fence and the trailer was gone, which wasn't particularly unusual, since Clarence had been let out on bail to set his affairs in order. But it kept nagging at me." He pulled a pouch from his pocket and handed me his pipe. "Do you know how to fill it? If not, you'd better start learning, woman."

I poured the tobacco into the bowl and, as I had seen him do so many times, tamped it down with my thumb. "I think you'll find me fairly intelligent and capable," I said with mock dignity. "Those are the qualifications you named in your letter to Dr. Burley, aren't they?"

"I think I mentioned trustworthiness, too," he said, deadpan. "Which was very discerning of me, don't you think, since you've had to fight, claw, starve, and even faint dead away in your efforts to save lives and restore order?"

"It was all worth it, now that we're going home," I told him. "I couldn't have endured another night away from Regent Manor."

Around us, the night fell silently and in the distance a light gleamed from a farmhouse. Danger was past and the future stretched before us like the highway of the padres who had made this Western country great.

Michael said from a puff of smoke, "When you said that you were going to Playland, I had my clue. If Gibbs were going to make his move, that would be the place for it—an accident, you know."

"Then it must have been he who gave Annette the ticket for the roller coaster."

"No doubt about it."

"I thought," I said, "that I saw him at the Fun House earlier, but I was a bundle of nerves and—this is silly—he was wearing dark glasses and he looked much taller."

"One of his disguises. He wouldn't be able to fool Annette otherwise, much as she detested him."

"So did you come straight to Playland?"

"At a hundred miles an hour! I checked out the Ferris wheel and merry-go-round, but I hesitated to get lost in the Fun House for fear I'd miss you. And then I checked the roller coaster and saw you two—and him. I spoke to the operator, but he had evidently been well paid by Gibbs. So without further ado, I called the beach police and told them there had been an accident—"

"—which hadn't actually taken place yet."

"No, but the plot was obvious—his seat close to yours, the proximity."

"Michael, my dear," I breathed, "you are a genius! Like the great archangel, you seem always to be on hand to defend me in my battle with the enemy."

"Be that as it may," he said indulgently, his hand closing over mine, "I'll be on hand for a long, long time. I don't expect ever to let you out of my sight again. By the way, I told Aunt Marian about us."

"And what did she say?" I asked eagerly.

"She didn't seem too much surprised." He gave me a comical look. "Did you two cook this up, maybe?"

"Oh, what male vanity!" I teased. "I wouldn't have had you as a gift studded with gems."

"Nor I, you. And look at us now." He pulled to the side of the country road and tipped my chin up to his face. "I've been wanting to kiss you for the last hour," he said, and did most satisfactorily. We sat in the moonlight listening to the night song of the cicadas, and Michael said dreamily, "Aunt Marian was up to her ears in wedding plans when I left. She pictures you in a cloud of white drifting down the Manor stairway into my waiting arms."

"I've had the same dream," I said, "only, not quite so magnificent. Will you mind the fuss too much, darling? She never saw Sylvia married, and Annette's is a long time away."

"No, I don't mind," he said, kissing me again. "I rather fancy myself in striped trousers and tailcoat. I hope you ask that fool, Charles, so he can see that the best man always wins."

"Egotist!"

"How about tomorrow? Next week? Why not? All you need is a white dress and a bunch of flowers."

It was nonsense, light and loving, but there was a stronger current, too, of foreverness. I had come to Regent Manor, a homeless nurse on a simple case, and I had come to stay.